A Painted Moment

by Jennifer Ching

Proverse Hong Kong

The sakura have fallen and frost is gaining ground. Yun, Rachel's best friend has died, and she is at a loss. With his passing, she mourns the fabric of their friendship and the eternal warmth of his family. Heading back to the island for the funeral are some of their oldest and closest friends; Chloe, a repressed perfectionist, and Olivia, golden child, both of whom she will grieve with and seek solace in. Along with their consolations, they bring with them their own issues and anger, dredging up buried fissures in their history. The time of their reunion also becomes a time of questioning, as they measure the choices they have made and wonder at the happy ending they each seek. And finally, lost in the folds of the past, Rachel is haunted by memories and confronted by the need to forge her own future. **A Painted Moment** is a story of friends, forgiveness and the paths we walk in life.

About the Author
Jennifer Ching was brought up and for the most part schooled in Hong Kong. She spent three years in London at fashion school, followed by a year working for a dotcom company, writing to user communities online. Jennifer spends most of her spare time traveling, sharing a drink with friends, or reading. Her favourite writers include David Mitchell, Aaron Sorkin and Agatha Christie. She lives in Hong Kong and works for a large American broadcast network.

Supported by

Hong Kong Arts Development Council

The Hong Kong Arts Development Council fully supports freedom of artistic expression. The views and opinions expressed in this project do not represent the stand of the Council.

A Painted Moment

Jennifer Ching

Proverse Hong Kong

A Painted Moment
by Jennifer Ching.
5th ed. published in pbk in Hong Kong by Proverse Hong Kong,
January 2018
Copyright © Proverse Hong Kong, January 2018.
ISBN: 978-988-8491-32-2

1st pub. in pbk in Hong Kong by Proverse Hong Kong, March 2010.
ISBN 978-988-18905-1-1
Copyright © Proverse Hong Kong, March 2010.

Distribution and other enquiries to Proverse Hong Kong,
P.O. Box 259, Tung Chung Post Office,Tung Chung, Lantau Island,
New Territories, Hong Kong SAR.
E-mail: <proverse@netvigator.com>. Web: <proversepublishing.com>

Front and back cover artwork and cover design by Kendra Wan.
www.kendrawan.com
~~~

Moral Rights: The right of Jennifer Ching to be identified as the author of this
work has been asserted by her in accordance with the Copyright, Designs and
Patents Act 1988. The right of Stuart Christie to be identified as the author of
"Review" has been asserted by him in accordance with the Copyright, Designs
and Patents Act 1988.

Proverse Hong Kong

British Library Cataloguing in Publication Data (1st edition)

Ching, Jennifer.
A painted moment.
1. Best friends--Death--Fiction. 2. Reunions--Fiction.
3. Choice (Psychology)--Fiction.
I. Title II. Bickley, Gillian
823.9'2-dc22

ISBN-13: 9789881890511

A rare first novel

Jennifer Ching's A Painted Moment is that rare first novel which presents an ensemble of characters convincingly and with a delicacy that speaks of even better writing to come. The novel opens to the shattering blow received by Rachel Glass, the young owner of a small-town independent book store, upon hearing of the sudden death of her friend and lover, Yun Ung. Like her name, Rachel's fragility and grief is transparent to all. Yung's death and pending funeral invokes the necessary and ritual reunion of Rachel and Yun's wider circle of friends since childhood. Once the group reassembles, the old passions and grievances resurface, tempered by a common absence which recasts the forgotten joys and simmering anger only long-standing fellowship knows. The island mists, crossings, and departing ferries Ching offers as the background to her story of rekindled friendship could be those of Victoria, British Columbia, or even perhaps a more temperate version of Hong Kong's own archipelago.

A lesser writer could easily have lost control with the pitch of emotion such a story requires, with too much sentiment casting off plausibility. But Ching's voice is measured and controlled when re-crafting otherwise merely conventional signposts of a life. In A Painted Moment, such conventions attending character -- grief, transformation, rebirth -- are written with a poise and distinction which affirm the truth that life-changing events may happen to others conventionally, but they are strikingly and devastatingly unique when they happen to us. Personal without being mawkish, A Painted Moment hits virtually all of its notes superbly.

One specific device Ching uses most effectively. This is a meandering parable, in form of a story Yun used to tell Rachel, specific elements of which inhabit each of the novel's three sections. This parable progresses apart from the story the novel tells, even as it is integral of the story's substance. In the parable, a lonely little girl, Lan, is awakened to the pleasures of her playful shadow by an old stranger her family befriends. She grows into young adulthood happily, only to discover that with maturity her shadow, her youthful companion, has deserted her. Or has it?

The parable is a finely wrought gem, a compact but not dense version of the lesson Rachel herself must learn about living without Yun: that the fear and grief attending profound loss may be compensatory, for a time, but they are no substitute for the continuation of life. Death, after all, is not and cannot be a monument to itself, but to life. In Ching's own words, irrevocable loss may be "an unbearable morning greeting", but we persevere, most persevere, through the heat of the afternoon and, if we yet have hope, into the twilight of an evening. And A Painted Moment is one such story of perseverance, of getting through the hardships of the morning. It is also about the age-old theme that never, after all, gets old -- of youth sacrificed to wisdom.

Finally, I like Rachel and Yun because I believed in them, not only as characters but as people that I might have liked to meet or, even, to become. I respected Rachel's grief and, in my view, that is the great achievement of Ching's novel. She has reminded me of the dignity of grief as a process and as an event from which none of us is exempt and all too few of us recover. Yet, exit from grief we must, else we become an island shade, limited to shadows, fearful of the light, fearful of life. And there is no glory or satisfaction in the retreat from life.

In the work of Jennifer Ching, Hong Kong has found a new and welcome voice in fiction. And, as one among the many worlds well-chosen words create, A Painted Moment is a slender, but significant, novel. In it, the sum total of human experience pushes forward a fraction, inclining immeasurably (if perceptibly) towards the light. There is growth, there is being, there will be a tomorrow. I look forward to Ms Ching's next novel unreservedly.

Stuart Christie, HKADC Literary Arts Examiner

A Painted Moment

Contents

Characters in order of appearance

Yun Ung

Recently deceased, best friend and pillar of wisdom to Rachel Glass. Of Chinese descent, brother to Ang Ung. Wise for his years, kind, loyal, a story-teller with an offbeat sense of humour. He arrived on the island with his family when he was six years old, so was one of the strongest links in the group. He was very attached to Rachel and saw it his mission to make her life easier and lighter. His death sets off the gathering of friends on their home island.

Rachel Glass

Main character and narrator of the story. Only child, her parents are retired and living in a small town off the island, so she runs their family business, a book-store called The Three Wisemen, on her own. Rachel is timid, soft-spoken, thoughtful, deferential and mostly passive. She was born on the island and therefore knows everyone and their stories, but her character has never been strong enough to ignite one of her own. She has never had a romantic relationship of significance. She mostly lives through the lives of her other friends. At the beginning of the story, she is grieving over the loss of Yun, whom she helped take care of throughout his last months.

Uncle Ung

Yun's father. Chinese. Passionate about photography, retired, energetic. Had a falling out with Ang, his elder son, and drove him away. Yun inherited his stories from him. Death of Yun has weakened him to the point of emotional zombification.

Aunt Ung

Yun's mother. Chinese. Elgant, competent, composed and wise. Wears elegant cheong sams and has a tendency to feed everyone in the neighbourhood. She is the strongest character in the family, and indeed in the book.

Chloe

Childhood friend. Organised, critical, driven, perfectionist, slightly judgmental. Was slightly chubby when she was young, hence the nickname 'Chubs'. Abused by her mother when she was young and has been estranged from her father since University. Was Sylvain's childhood sweetheart until the day her mother abandoned her and her father. Fell out with Olivia over a scholarship and Will, just before University and has never let go. Fiercely protective of Rachel. At the beginning of the story, her illicit relationship with a married man has been discovered. As a result of that discovery, she is fired from an illustrious job at a city newspaper.

Olivia

Childhood friend. Gracious, intelligent, beautiful, wealthy, ironic with a generous heart. Born to wealthy and professionally driven parents, life has always come to her easily. Is frustrated by Chloe's anger and would love to reconnect. Married William, a successful writer with whom she had a whirlwind romance, while still at University. Views Rachel with affectionate amusement and love. At the beginning of the story, she has just found out she is pregnant and is contemplating leaving William.

Glory
Childhood friend. Anxious, well meaning and motherly. Married to Josh. The couple run a coffee shop on the same street as The Three Wisemen. She has never been on the same wavelength as the other girls and therefore has never been as close to the girls as she would like to be. The life she leads is comfortable and uneventful but she is content with that.

Josh
Childhood friend. Dependable, straightforward, practical and unadventurous. Was in the year above the rest of the group and so is not at the core of the friendship circle. Closest to James Aimes out of the whole group. Has no spare thoughts. Like his wife, he is content with his lot.

Sylvain
Childhood friend. Smart and quick, moodily tempered, secretly sentimental. A successful but almost reluctant banker in the city, a job he took to please his family. Used to dream of travel. Never got over Chloe and is subconsciously hoping that she will one day return to him. At the beginning of the story, his success at his job is not enough to assuage him of the idea that he should really be living another life.

Amherst
Childhood friend. Quirky, artistic, free spirited. Jazz afficiando. Forever on the outskirts of the little group, as he never quite fits in anywhere.

James Aimes
Childhood friend. Snide, slightly arrogant and overbearing. The last to arrive at their school on the island from the city. Runs his own press distribution company.

Ang Ung
Brother to Yun. Left town after an argument with his father. Free spirit.

9

Dedication

To my "tribe" — loved ones, friends and family.

Yun

In every life.

There is always a moment when what once was, is no longer, and what will come is not yet clear. Yun says we are positioned that way, fraught with possibility, rich with potential, caught like the moment when Clark Kent runs into the phone booth, before he bursts out in a glory of muscle and red underwear. Or maybe those nature documentaries of caterpillars trapped in a cocoon, pulsating a pea green and visible through a thin cataract film. Perhaps. Before our eyes can dance a thousand futures, however briefly, until dancing shadows slide and melt into one nebulous form, leaving us blind-sighted and gasping in its tantalizing wake. We can spend our lives holding our breath, eyes unblinking, on the cusp, until we realize with a violent shock that it's behind us. Memories resemble flashbulbs bursting in the dark of our peripheral consciousness, throwing light on one gesture, a remembered sequence, a tilt of the head. A pause in yesterday's conversation, a door never opened, buttered with the haze of hindsight. Trailing hangnail of fog enveloping moored boats as we turn in our sleep, a mimicked existence amongst clouds. We are all poised that way. Walking barefoot to the very end of a pier spanning the water, the soft powder blue of the sky on the water's horizon, an azure that makes my eyes water.

"Have you heard the one about the two priests and the bartender?"

I looked up from absentmindedly tracing the patterns on his quilted bedspread. There were barely perceptible gold threads twisted and burnt to form the lines that wove their way through the rich padded silk. I had one too, Aunt Ung had made sure to quilt me one shortly after Yun received his. Mine was a colourful patchwork of purple, green and gold. Yun's was a dark blue, a strong tall oak at its centre and a host of blinking owls perched on its branches. We used to have stories about all twelve of the owls but I no longer remembered them all.

"Yes."

Yun propped his book open on his chest, the back of his head resting on the headboard. We were reading Marquez's *One Thousand Years of Solitude* together, Marquez was one of his favourite writers. His thin face was flushed and his eyes were almost feverishly bright, like he was mainlining adrenaline.

"What about the one about the three priests and the bartender?"

"That one too."

The owl near the bottom left hand corner, the one Aunt Ung had embroidered with a funny squint was nicknamed Oliver. Oliver for Yun's pet hamster that had drowned in a thunderstorm. Oliver for Yun's Labrador that had been put down when it was four. Constant namesake.

"Were they Irish, English and Scottish?"

I laughed.

"Yes, yes they were."

"Ah – now the one that I want to tell you about, the priests are Irish, English and Welsh."

"Yun, I don't want to sit here and listen to a joke about priests and bartenders."

"Why not? It's not going to be religious."

"That's the thing, I only like religious jokes."

"Bull."

"I have to go soon," I said keeping a straight face, "Will you be alright?"

"Without you?" Yun smiled, "I'll be fine. Will you be?"

"I think so", I answered, not entirely convinced myself. I never liked to travel.

You've been so brave, he said. It's not about being brave, I replied, the owls gently rearranging themselves across the bed as I got up. You're right, it's not about that, but that's what you are. The egg yolk yellow of the sun had yielded to a crimson dye, setting everything afire, casting eerie shadows on the long wood floor. I reached over and gave Yun a tight hug, my head on his shoulder, my laughter spirited away by a paralysing ache. He smoothed the back of my hair and I sensed him breathing in the scent of my skin. When I tried to do the same, I thought I could still smell him underneath the burn of plastic capsules. Then he kissed me on the forehead and shooed me away.

So I went. I packed and repacked, took the ferry out across the water, got into a cab, double-checking the address I'd scribbled hastily in my organizer. The cab drew up to a neat, white washed, fairly non-descript building; as it drew away, the hind wheel splashed water from a small puddle onto my boots. Chloe had informed me of this approaching "great seminar" and that "it would help the Wiseys".
"I wasn't under the impression that we needed help", I'd answered lightly.
"That's not the point. He's great – and I hear, very good looking."
"So that's the point?"
"Why must there be a point?"
"There always is a point, with you."
"Fine, yes you may have a point, well this would be quite the case of killing two birds with one stone. Or so I hope."
"You've not met him personally?" I asked, thumb and forefinger rubbing in between my eyebrows.
"Who needs to meet him? You do – not me. Don't argue, just go. It'll be good for you to get off that bloody island."
I started to argue that I was happy where I was, but as usual, up against Chloe's logic, conviction and ferocious determination, I was quite simply unable. I shifted my shoulder bag to the other side. So I found myself standing in the lobby of this neat, white washed, fairly non-descript building, a ferry and cab journey away from Yun. Above my head hung a slightly droopy, multi-coloured Merry Christmas banner, the "E" of which was hanging on to the rest of the letters within an inch of its life. Muted classical music played in the background and I had the sensation of being on the set for a television show.
"Merry Christmas."
I turned my head to regard a neat, rather non-descript man sitting behind the reception counter. He might have had silver framed glasses and a pen in his front pocket. The shirt might have been striped.

"It's just gone November", I replied, surmising that the banner must have been there since last Christmas.

"Our customers enjoy the Christmas cheer", came the response.

I stood there wordlessly for a moment (What to say?) until inspiration seemed to seize him.

"Tips for Modern Survival?" He asked.

I nodded.

"Function Room 1 to your left but most people left about ten minutes ago," The man said, "The entourage are still in there though, so if you hurry, you may still be able to catch a few pearls of wisdom, as I'm guessing you need it." Having pronounced this infuriating assumption, he turned back to the television he had been watching before I interrupted his uneventful life.

Cursing the man under my breath, I rushed down the hall and through the doors of Function Room 1, where I was stopped.

"Just one minute, sweetheart, just hold on. We're finishing up here." A tall, tan woman in a pressed cream suit held out one hand in my direction, the other hand hovering above a group of seated people. Vaguely, her blonde perfection reminded me of Chloe. The room was box sized, with an odd backdrop on the furthest wall, something of cheap red velvet and fluorescent lights that flickered above.

"Now, I'd like you all to take a moment to recognize the positive energy in the room. Breathe in and feel that energy running into your lungs and flushing out all the toxins in your system. Yes, now breathe with me." The woman made a beckoning motion as the group, eyes closed, took a collective deep breath. Someone coughed. I advanced forward and perched gingerly on a chair a few rows behind the groupies, unsure of what to do.

"Now open your eyes. You feel refreshed and alive. Cast your mind back to everything we've been talking about. Money is the driving force in this world, there's a fair share of it out there in the universe and it's your prerogative to earn a large portion of it. You can do it! So get up and make some money!" The woman brought her hands together and flashed the group a bright, white smile. The people sitting in front of her, one or two of them variously leaping to their feet, gave her a round of enthusiastic applause. It was like *Return of the Living Dead. 2.*

"Thank you, thank you for being such brilliant students. If you think you might be interested in the next seminar, pick up some leaflets on your way out. It will be about becoming a modern day warrior in business!" She waved her perfectly manicured fingernails at her loyal students before turning to me. A girl with thick glasses got up with a book in hand as if waiting for a signature.

"Now, hello sweetheart. Running a bit late are we?" She half turned to sign the book. My mouth was still hanging open from her little speech.

"I'm actually here to see a Dr Morris Fenwick", I finally managed, trying to choke back a horrified laugh.

"Yes, that would be me." The whiteness of her teeth was really beginning to hurt my eyes, "And I'm here to help! Now, you run a small business?"

"Erh – well, Dr Fenwick," I faltered, making a mental note to kill Chloe, "I –".

"That's perfectly alright dear, you can talk to me." She dismissed the groupie and clasped her hands in front of her.

I had never found it easy, opening up to people I didn't know, much less an immaculate peroxide Scrooge. For a moment, I entertained the desire to run, but like a fox on the scent of a rabbit, Dr Fenwick took me by the crook of my arm and ushered me to another group of chairs. We sat and she crossed her legs, propping an arm up on one knee, one finger held thoughtfully up. I cleared my throat. No way out now. Maybe she was better than she looked. I cleared my throat again.

I began by telling her about Wiseys, but no sooner had the word book-store left my mouth did Dr Morris Fenwick let out a peal of laughter and the few people still in the room cocked their ears curiously.

"Sweetheart therein lies your problem. Books are dinosaurs! On their way out! Extinct! Dead! "

I made to cut in but the woman bulldozed on regardless.

"FOSSILS. Past their sell by date. I wouldn't even advise you to do an Amazon at this critical stage", Dr Morris Fenwick pronounced dramatically.

"I actually think we're doing quite well," I said slowly, "I'm not sure how much you know about the book business, but I wouldn't say we're dead, just yet." I resented having to defend Wiseys. And I resented the time I was wasting on this woman.

"You are obviously a sentimental person," Dr Morris Fenwick sighed, "But if your little bookshop was doing so well, would you really be here?"

I began to tell her how I came to be in what I increasingly realized was the wrong situation but she would have none of it.

"Take my advice and toss aside this sentiment." She mimed screwing my 'sentiment' into a paper ball and tossed it over her shoulder – here, the last two stragglers of the group burst into applause again. She smiled winningly and brushed a non-existent stray hair from her forehead with the edge of her nail. I made another mental note to kill Chloe, checking the exits and waiting for a break in her speech so I could make my getaway.

"Sweetheart, have you ever thought about going into a different field? An industry you can see a future in? Like – *biotechnology?*" Her hands painted an abstract future in the air." Let me tell you how you can take a hold of your career by the horns and turn it around."

She put her taloned hand around my arm and all hope of flight was extinguished.

Forty-five minutes later, I emerged from Function Room 1 in desperate need of some fresh air. I fell through the glass doors and into the brisk night air. My breath made white clouds in the air and I rubbed my arms to warm them. I could not believe I had come for this, I should have known better. Fleetingly, I thought I might be able to hop on the last ferry home, but then realized I was too late. In the blue black night, I could make out white and yellows that flecked and twinkled sporadically, dot blob dot. If only. But. With another resigned breath, I headed back inside. Approaching the reception, I eyed the man behind it warily. Ostentatiously, he was still watching television, one of the endless cycles of bad eighties operas with their own dedicated intravenously-fed channel and audience.

"Hello."

The man made a show of realizing I was standing in front of the counter, bag in hand.

"Ah. Yes. You."

"Yes, me. I have a room reservation, under the name Glass, just for one night."

"Good seminar? Modern Tips for Survival?" He asked me as he lazily scanned his guest book.

I didn't answer.

The man reached under the counter and retrieved the door card. He stood there, door card in hand. I realized he was expecting me to respond.

"I'm tired," I said flatly, "I'd really like some peace and quiet."

"Payment upon checkout, Ms Glass. Sweet dreams", he said, handing it to me.

Thankful I had only my overnight bag, I crossed the lift lobby and pressed the lift call-button. The elevator doors creaked as they opened, I looked behind me as I stepped into the lift. The non-descript man had already turned back to the television, a barely perceptible buzzing sound betraying its age.

The room was clean in a beige, spare way, with a beige bed in the middle of the room, beige curtains at the windows and a mirrored sliding door on a beige closet. I dumped my bag, lifted the curtains to check the non-view. I took up the remote control and channel-surfed for a while, my legs stretched out far in front of me. A two hundred pound woman was being interviewed by a reed thin man, who seemed oblivious to the fact that she was crying. The audience was booing them loudly, but neither the two hundred pound woman nor the thin man seemed to care. Change channels. Re-run of *Sleepless in Seattle*, a movie I neither liked nor could bring myself to deride. I searched the mini-fridge and briefly contemplated getting drunk, turning the tiny bottles over in my hand. Chloe's voice popped into my head. I stuck the bottles back into the fridge. I wondered at people who reveled in the anonymity of hotel rooms, just like the one I was in now. I tried to imagine the occupant of the room beneath mine, standing or sleeping. Alone or not. It got under my skin, the way wool blankets scratched. Sitting on the bed, I rifled through my bag, realizing that I had probably brought too much with me and despite my repacking, I had left my mobile at home. I dug up Yun's dog-eared copy of *The Motorcycle Diaries* and climbed into bed with my clothes still on.

I woke to the shrieking in a re-run of *Psycho*.

For a moment, my skin prickled with apprehension as I cast about, disorientated. The book had slipped from my hand and the phone on the bedside-table was ringing.

"Hello?" My voice cracked.

"Hello Ms Glass, this is reception calling."

I shivered in the controlled temperature of the room, my legs cramping.

"Is there something the matter?" I squinted at the bedside clock. It was three in the morning.

"I didn't want to disturb you, as Ms Glass specified she was tired and wanted some peace and quiet, but you have a call and the caller is rather insistent that he should speak to you." There was the faint trace of smugness in his words.

"Thank you," I said patiently, "For your thoughtfulness. Can you put the person through?"

"Certainly."

He pressed a button and immediately a different background noise crowded down the line, muffled voices, babies crying. Something in the sound of the footsteps echoing down a long hall-way knocked the last cobweb of sleep from my head. And then Yun's father spoke.

On our island, sakura floats on the air, fairy lights cling to Christmas trees lining the road and we dance for the lady on the moon during lantern festivals. Aunt Ung wraps fresh wonton every Sunday and we eat these with long, ivory chopsticks, cool to the touch.

"Have you heard the one about the genie and the three wishes?"
I started from my half sleep and crossed the room to his bedside in two strides, banging my hip on the metal bed frame, the harsh smell of disinfectant making my nostrils flare. Yun slowly smiled at me with dry lips.
I made to pass him a glass of water but he shook his head.
"Have you?"
I nodded my head.
"Really? I must have told you that one. That one was quite good."
His voice was hoarse and very soft.
I dipped my fingers in the glass of water and reached out to moisten his lips.
"Why don't you tell me a joke then, since you know all of mine?"
"You know I'm no good at jokes."
"What about a story?"
"You're the story-teller, not me."
"I would love to hear you tell me a story."
Alright then. A story, a story. What about the story your mother used to tell us when we were young, the one about the girl and her shadow? I remember. Would you like me to tell it? If you wouldn't mind. No, of course I wouldn't, how could I mind? I suppose to start *there once was a little girl named Lan, who lived with her parents up in the mountains, where winter comes early and spring comes late. Her mother sewed for a living and her father charged travelers for taking them up and down the mountain on his donkey-driven carriage. Although her parents loved her, Lan could get terribly lonely, because there was never anyone around to play with her. One day, on a particularly bitter night, her father had still to return; Lan and her mother were sitting in front of the hearth, warming their hands around bowls of congee and red beans, and worrying for the father's safety. Lan's mother was about to suggest that she get into bed when the door to their small cottage blew open with the force of a thousand gales of wind. Standing framed in the doorway was her father and a stranger wrapped in a dark cloak.*
"Who have you brought into our house?" cried Lan's mother, jumping back.

A Painted Moment

"He was my passenger this evening, but he collapsed half way up the mountain and I didn't want to leave him alone outside", said Lan's father.

"You don't know who he is. Are you sure we should take him in?"

"If we don't take him in, he'll die out there", Lan's father responded firmly." Let's put him somewhere warm."

Together, they carried the stranger over by the fire, laid him down and covered him with a blanket. At first, Lan couldn't see the stranger's face as her parents fussed over him, but later, she saw that he was an old man, with a long white beard and moustache. At first he dozed fitfully but then he fell into a deep sleep, tended by Lan's mother. In the morning, when Lan woke, she heard noises coming from outside her room. Rushing out, she saw that the stranger was up and well again, and in fact sitting at their dining-table eating breakfast with her parents. When the old man saw her, he smiled at her and beckoned for her to sit next to him.

"What is your name, little one?" he asked, even though she was sure her parents had already told him. He had a deep voice that Lan liked instantly, so she told him. The two fell into conversation, and Lan told him everything she could think of about their family. Lan's parents went about their daily tasks, while the two of them talked. She told him how poor they were, how hard her father worked and how her mother's fingers ached on cold nights. She told him what it was like not to eat chicken or have new clothes to wear during the New Year. Most importantly, she told him how lonely she was and how she longed to have a sister or a friend. The stranger didn't say very much; he merely listened and nodded his head; but he had a thoughtful expression on his face as he tugged at his long beard. When Lan had run out of things to say to him, he leaned forward till his nose was just inches from Lan's.

"I have a secret to share with you, Lan", he said softly, his eyes twinkling, "But you must promise not to tell anyone."

Excited, Lan held her breath, waiting to hear what the secret was.

"What would you do, if you had a friend to play with all day long, who would take care of you, be loyal to you for as long as you needed?"

Lan's face shone with excitement. That was the only response the stranger needed.

I stopped. Yun's eyes opened.

"Go on", he whispered, putting his hand in mine.

I clutched his hand tightly.

So the stranger gave Lan a kiss on her forehead, patted her hand, creakily got up, and left the cottage. Lan chased after him, watched him hobble off down the mountain, his beard fluttering in the wind. Where is my friend? She wanted to cry but she balled her hands into little fists and bit back a disappointed shout. As she turned to go back into the house, her shadow cast itself across the ground and then it waved at her. Surprised, Lan jumped back, but her shadow didn't move with her. Instead, her shadow kept waving and then started to dance around like a monkey would. Now delighted, Lan stuck out her hand and her shadow reached out and held it; hand in hand, the two walked away.

***

"It's so small."

"Getting smaller."

"I feel like I've forgotten something", Chloe bites her lip.

"Stop worrying Chubs", Yun sighs, shading his eyes from the sun.

"Don't call me that", Chloe snaps.

Ordinarily, I would laugh, but I can't seem to find the lightness in my heart. As we watch, the island is fading into the distance.

"You need to start college with a new name", Yun says in his most facetious voice, plopping down in a striped deck chair, stretching out his legs, his arms folded behind his head. Chloe shoots him a dirty look and starts rooting through her bag.

"You two are the only ones that still use it!"

I'm leaning over the ferry railings as the two bicker behind me. Chloe's voice has taken on a slightly clipped accent, affected remnants of a few weeks stay in London during the holidays. The ferry deck is busy and noisy with running children and romancing lovers. Despite the sun, the September wind whipping my hair brings out the goose bumps on my arms and stings my eyes. She has also taken to saying "quite", a habit she will never entirely be rid of.

"Don't worry, it will still be there when you come back." Yun pokes my leg, one eye squinting as he gazes up at me.

"I just can't believe we're going to college", I say simply, looking down at him.

"Rache, we've been through this before, you'll have a grand time." Chloe is still sifting, her attention elsewhere.

Yun rests his head against my thigh.

"It will be Christmas in a blink of an eye," He says kindly, "Oli's been gone for two months already and it hasn't seemed like very long has it?"

Chloe's chin tilts upwards a little as she stops rummaging.

"We've talked about her quite enough", she states, mutinous.

Yun sighs, running a hand through his hair. Chloe meets our eyes defiantly, finally fishing out a pair of sunglasses and putting them on. Her newly cropped hair clusters close to her head, setting off her cheekbones in a surprisingly flattering way. She had it cut the day after the scholarship results came out, making the decision to lop off her waist-length hair without a second thought. Gone is the old Chloe and in her place is a sleek imposter, eager to leave her old disappointments and pain behind. I can't help but eggshell my way around her, not quite sure where the new cracks are located.

"What I mean is, it will fly by", Yun supplements diplomatically, not willing to take sides, spreading out his hands as he has been doing for years.

"How do you know for sure?" I challenge him.

"How do you know for sure?" He counters, "It's a new slate, fresh blood."

He grabs me round the knees, forcing me to sit on the edge of his chair.

"New men, at least", Chloe laughs, climbing over Yun to take the chair next to his.

Yun snorts. Chloe reaches out to punch him on the arm and the two start mock fighting right there on the deck, Yun with one hand on Chloe's forehead, keeping her an arm's length away. With a pang, I wonder what Olivia is doing then, ensconced in her new dorm room, her window open to the maple and bronze topped trees, surrounded by other scholarship kids, fellow luminaries. I can still see the look of pain on Chloe's face when the announcement was made, Olivia's mouth dropping open first with pleasure and then with helpless guilt as Chloe quickly steps away. With hindsight, one can always trace back to the exact moment when something starts to go wrong.

"You can become a new person", Yun goes on, collapsing back, slightly out of breath, Chloe busy sorting out her hair, her eyes unreadable behind her big sunglasses.

I tuck a stray strand of hair behind one ear and am aware of how beat up my converse are, how much the sun and water has bleached the original beige colour. I don't want to become a new person.

Yun, reading my mind, looks me square in the face, his eyes twinkling. Hope is golden, with an effervescent dusting floating on the air. When I look at Yun, he seems set apart, precious to the touch and I know I will remember this scene for years to come.

"You get to write your own ending, Rachel", excitement in his quiet voice." The ending to your own story, how would you write that?"

Caught up in the potential of his dreams, I flush, unsteady with the possibilities. What would I write? Then a whistle sounds, it is almost time to get off, near our destination. I turn my head back quickly, hitting my forehead on the railing. Too late. The island has already disappeared from my horizon.

A Painted Moment

Part One
Loss is an unbearable morning greeting

The sky simpered.

Yun rapped gently against the window. Let me in, it's raining out. With a start, I woke to a tapping sound, like footsteps running across our rooftop. Rats. Cats. Robbers. My eyes strayed to the tennis racquet sticking out of my wardrobe before I realized mildly through a misty haze of sleep that it was raining. Whenever it rained, I always thought of the movie *Cat on a Hot Tin Roof* for no reason I could fathom, maybe less to do with the movie than the idea of cats prancing on rooftops.

From under heavy lids, the sky beyond the window looked a watered down grey, an early morning palette of clouds blended into the nothingness of the background. On the edge of what might have been a dream were the frayed edges of the ocean and the bitter after taste of salt on my tongue. I pulled the duvet over my head, trying to shut out the noise, breathing in and out so that a hot air bubble was trapped in there with me.

Still, the rain came down.

Finally convinced that I wasn't going to get any more sleep, I rolled out of bed, studied the shape of my knees for as long as I could before heading for the bathroom, padding on the ends of my pajama pants. On my way, my toe connected with the tennis racquet and a sharp pain ran up the length of my leg. Clenching my left fist round it, I hopped for the bathroom, a stream of profanities marking my path. Kneeling on the bathroom floor, I counted to ten as the throbbing set in before I unclenched. Nail intact, dark maroon had begun to spread from the base of the nail upwards. Leaning in as close as I could I touched the ridges across the surface of the nail, thinking briefly the dark maroon was actually closer to a plum. Being careful not to hurt my toe any more, I leant forward to turn on the shower, let the water run through my fingers. I caught sight of my pale face in the mirror – tangle of hair and an expression that I could hardly name – I averted my eyes. Somewhere between pain and the baptismal rush of the water, I teetered, eyes shut against the blue of the wall tiles. I experimented with holding my breath for as long as I could, gradually phasing out any sensation but the drumming against my skull, the pressure against my nostrils only to gulp in a mouthful of water with my next panicked breath. A truly failed experiment. Rubbing a soggy circle in the centre of the fogged mirror, I searched past my reflection, tried to imagine a message left for me in the mirror. What would it say and did it matter how long I stood here for? I toweled off and cast around for something to wear, it seemed the faster I performed tasks these days, the easier it was to get through the day, like I could leave the pain behind in a blur but what I was instead left with was too much time. Limping a little, I pulled on a pair of worn jeans that were hanging over a chair and a thick, autumn coloured sweater. Before leaving my room, I shoved the offending tennis racquet back into the closet and slid the door firmly shut, asking myself when the last time I played tennis was. The emptiness of the house gave me momentary pause, as, unbidden, flashed images of lanterns lining a path in the otherwise pitch dark, gravel being kicked up and laughter. I waited for the images to recede before I negotiated the dark hall-ways with one hand to the wall, trailing a path from my room past the guest rooms, the study, the storage closet, till the curve to my touch opened out to the living-room on the left and the dining room on the right, sombre and unused. Tucked and rolled almost under one corner of our large leather sofa was a dark red oriental rug, banished to languish for as long as it reminded me of blood. From just inside the sliding glass doors of the kitchen porch, through the dining room, I could just see out over to the Ung's house shrouded in mist. There was a light on in one of the bedroom windows, but the rest of the house seemed sound asleep. I thought briefly of taking the hat over to Aunt Ung now, but then decided it was probably still too early. I was certain that she must wake with a sudden jolt, when her body didn't remember, her mind reeling to make sense, her heart a gaping yawn that refused to be filled. Loss was an unbearable morning greeting. I flinched involuntarily at the thought and had to turn away, a hand almost instinctively over my eyes. I stood a moment in the centre of the room, just breathing. I glanced again at the bright, smooth hat box but left it on the dining room table, unmoved.

I wound a red and white striped thick wooly scarf from Chloe ("People with no body-fat need to wear more clothes, I'm telling you, if you don't wear this after I spent umpteen hours knitting it....") round my neck, pulled on a jacket, grabbed my bag and stepped out the door. The smell of the rain in the pines caught me full in the face as I slid the heavy wooden doors together, listening for the click of the latch before I turned the key in the lock. The rain was as yet a misty, inconsistent drizzle, nothing dramatic yet.

"Isn't it beautiful? That smell? That sound?" Yun said. I almost turned to check. He loved the rain. Pink and purple stains on our seven year-old hands from the sakura laden with rainwater, rainwater fallen through the pines, released from an iron fisted sky. I almost turned to check.

Taking an umbrella from the stand by the door, I opened its bright canary shade into the drizzle, walking quickly, small pebbles kicked up in my wake, pinecones splintering underfoot. I heard the tram approaching before I reached the main road, so I quickened my pace, just managing to jump on before the whistle sounded and the tram continued along its rickety track. Shaking the umbrella a little, I hooked it onto the handle on the back of the wooden seat ahead of me. The tram came out of the bend in the woods and headed for the main part of the town, small square boxes of white and blue, placed like Lego pieces. Behind the town rose a cold majestic mountain range. A cool breeze lifted my hair lightly, so I did up the buttons of my jacket.

My bag, now resting in my lap shook almost imperceptibly. Sifting through it, my hands found the source of the disturbance.

"'Morning."

"Hi honey. How are you? What are you doing up this early?"

"On the tram into Wiseys. Rain woke me up, couldn't get back to sleep." On cue, the tram shook gently, turning a corner. "How are you? How's Dad?"

"Well, hot, but I shouldn't complain", Mum answered, pausing as someone muttered in the background, "Dad says hi."

"Hi back."

Mum asked if I had received the hat through the mail, her natural tendency being to distrust public service of any sort. I marveled at how the hat had traveled that many miles without any dent as testament.

"Actually, honey, we were calling about our flights", Mum said hesitantly.

"That doesn't sound too positive."

"Well, no. I suppose it isn't. We're on the waitlist. Everything's sold out, the travel agent says it's the Christmas season."

As if the travel agent must have the wisdom.

"Rachel. Honey?"

"Yeah, I'm here."

"The travel agent says there aren't any flights till after the New Year."

"It's the Christmas season", I echoed.

"I know but, well, we'll keep trying." She paused. Dad said something in the background again that mum didn't repeat. I had become used to dad talking behind mum since they have moved away.

"How's Aunt Ung?"

"Holding together, but just barely. Better than Uncle Ung anyway."

"I'll give her a ring. Make sure she's…well…I should really ring her."

There was nothing my mother could do to make sure Aunt Ung was alright, and she probably knew that.

"You do that."

"Rachel, honey."

"Mum."

"How are you?"

It was funny, like we'd gone full circle and started another conversation.

"You already asked me that."

"Yes, well, I know. But I'm asking for real this time."

"I could be better", I replied simply.

"You sound a little, well, better."

Not that much better.

The tram pulled into another stop where an old lady slowly got to her feet.

"Your dad and I were thinking. It's been a while since we all went on vacation together. Wouldn't it be nice to take a break", she added, "After all this is over?"

Small village walkways, white houses with old frangipani swaying on the air.

"I can't, mum. You know that. I couldn't be away from Wiseys for a week."

"Yes you can. You really need a vacation. You could come here, you haven't seen the house this year with its new coat of paint and the weather...."

"I'm fine, really I am."

"For us, baby, we miss you. Everyone will understand."

Who was everyone?

"I don't think so."

"Rachel."

"I'll call you later." Not waiting for a response, I cut the line and tossed the phone back into the bag, willing it not to ring again. For the next few minutes, I tried to push the conversation out of my head. Everyone will understand? What was that supposed to mean? Who was everyone and what did it matter to me if they understood or not? I glowered at my umbrella. The tram creaked around a corner, turning onto Wisey's road. I watched a family cross the street, a little girl and her parents. The little girl peered at me from under her bright sailor's rain hat, and then surreptitiously, she waved to me before her father swung her off the ground, avoiding a puddle. Olivia would love that little girl. What did she mean, everyone would understand? I asked myself again, as I pulled out my wallet. I passed it across the fare register panel on the top of the seat in front of me and rang the bell for my stop.

The local radio was playing in the background and the smell of coffee beans roasting rose to greet me as I pushed through the door of the coffee shop. Glory had her back to me, a maroon apron tied around her waist. At the sight of the umbrella stand just inside the door, I realized with a vehement curse that I'd left my umbrella on the tram.

"Hi Rache." She'd noticed me. Surprise. Surprise then turned into careful bewilderment. Carefully.

I stood there on the doormat, brushing raindrops off my coat, unsure of what to say.

"I haven't seen you in a while", Glory continued, her voice a little high pitched, her hands wringing her apron.

"I know", I ventured, "I haven't been – I've just been – you know, in and out a lot."

I tried a smile that ended up feeling more like a grimace. I moved the newspapers out of the way and plunked my bag on one of the long wooden tables. We regarded each other.

"Would you like some mint tea?" Glory asked.

"To go", I answered gratefully.

Glory turned to the many jars lining the back wall, pulling out one full of tea-leaves. She flicked on the heater below a large glass kettle filled with water, pushing a heavy curl out of the way with the back of her hand, a nervous gesture from childhood. I watched her pluck mint leaves off a potted mint plant and then crush them with a mortar and pestle. I pulled a long flask, wrapped in cloth, from my bag and set it on the counter. Trying for a semblance of nonchalance, I unfolded the papers and spread them open, searching absently for Chloe's column. It didn't appear to be there...*and that was, of course, U2...a great way to start the morning and now here's the weather report...* She spooned some honey into the mortar, briskly mixed in the mint and the tea-leaves. Reaching out to unscrew the flask, Glory cleared her throat determinedly.

"Rachel, I'm sorry about Yun."

I nodded too quickly, made a sound in my throat, not wanting to look at her directly. It was an intimacy that I had been trying to stay away from. Resolutely, I kept hunting for the column.

"How are you holding up?" She asked quietly, persistent.

Left with no choice, I finally looked her in the face, the words lost on my lips. I gave a convulsive shrug. What could I say? And from the heavy silence that followed, I supposed Glory was asking herself the same thing. We both watched the kettle, the water inside beginning to simmer. *Cold northern winds and heavy rain forecast for the next few days.* I glanced down at the newspaper on the table, the lead story of which was a scandal at a news agency, as she now poured the water from the kettle into the flask. The words swam in front of my eyes and I rubbed my temples. She screwed the cap back on the flask and slid it over to me where she stopped, hands clutched around it. I guessed she wanted to say something but was having a hard time forming the sentence. So despite what was by now a wild desire to bolt, I waited. Recent experience had taught me it was better to let someone say what was on their minds, lest it should fester and rot, and manifest itself elsewhere.

"I never expected it to be Yun," She said huskily, "You can never imagine something like that happening to people who are so...healthy."

Would it have made it any better if it were someone else?

"When Josh told me – he didn't want to tell me over the phone – he was crying." She shook her head. "I can't remember the last time I saw him cry. And then we were up all night, looking through the yearbook. It seemed like not so long ago, but that was what? Almost ten years. In just a blink of the eye."

It had been almost ten years. Almost.

"And then I remembered." The pitch of her voice rose slightly, "Ang".

Mildly surprised at the sharp turn in conversation, I looked at Glory. Why did she mention him? She was looking down now, wiping her hands on her apron, looking like she badly needed to say something but regretted the impulse at the same time.

"I don't mean to...", Glory faltered. "I mean, I...."

Mean to. No one ever means to.

At that moment though, my exit presented itself in the form of an elderly lady, a small wind chime announcing her arrival as she came through the door, the water from her umbrella already forming a small puddle on the floor.

Glory turned away and I could hear her taking deep breaths. I felt constricted in my own chest. I stuffed the flask back into my bag and slung it over my shoulder. I wanted to reach out to her, touch her shoulder, as much as I wanted to slink away and hide forever. So, I chose the coward's way out.

"I really should get going, Glory. I'll see you at dinner tonight", I said quietly. She nodded, mute, as she took another breath to steady herself.

I might have pushed past the elderly lady in my haste to get out of the door, leaving Glory standing behind the counter like an island left behind by a departing ship. Thirty seconds in the light rain like a burst of fresh air between Glory's gloom and Wiseys. Another heavy key in the old fashioned lock, the clear ring of the wind chimes – all the shops on the island had the same ones – as I fell through the doorway, closing the door firmly behind me, kicking up mail piled just inside the door, breathing in the comfort of my own place, the familiar taste and texture of Wiseys. So my first attempt at face-to-face normalcy had not gone so well. I hoped there was no way but up from here. I walked round the deep, rounded dark oak table that served as part register counter, part workspace. Reaching forward, I pulled lightly on the switch of the antique tiffany lamp on the table, next to the cash-register. Clearing a space amidst my loosely stacked papers, random newspaper clippings and books, I set down my tea and absently sorted through the mail – catalogues, bills, a business card with the words CALL ME printed across it in thin black marker, NATHAN BROOKS, PUBLISHING – I tossed it all into one pile, laid my hands flat on the table, steadying my breath. Some days, this oak table felt like a centre of gravity, if I laid my ear to its surface, I felt I could hear the earth tilt. My eyes fell on a blank notepad at the top of the stack, its starkness glowing in contrast, churning me with a sense of panicked reminder. Yun's eulogy. Still unwritten. And the funeral in less than twenty-four hours. Attempting to take my mind off it, I was deciding to take off my shoes when my bag shook again. Reaching over, I glanced at the caller ID on my phone.

"Hi, Chloe."

"Is it raining over there?" I could hear shrill city sounds, almost drowning out half of her sentence.

"Yes, it is", I answered, plumping down into a squishy armchair and bending over to untie my converse, "And it's cold."

"Perfect. Listen, I just wanted to ask what the arrangements for the next few days are."

"Arrangements?" I echoed, "For Yun's big bash?" I yanked off my left shoe.

"That's not quite what I meant, Rache", Chloe sighed. "I just don't want to do my usual thing when I get in because you'll get all irritated. I know you have a lot on your mind."

"We have dinner tonight at seven. We're meant to be at the cemetery at two tomorrow and then over to his parents' place for the wake." I pulled off the other shoe and straightened up, shoe in hand. "Everyone's going to be there."

"Syl's already on the ferry back", Chloe added as if in justification. "He called to tell me."

"That's very prompt of him", I said.

"Quite. For once in his life, he's early. He used never to be on time." The words when we were dating hung unspoken.

I stood up, flung my shoes into a corner and picked up my mug from a hook above a small sink in the corner. I unscrewed the top, pulled back the flap and filled my cup.

"So."

"I need to ask you."

"What?"

"How have you been sleeping?" Her voice was hesitant but firm.

"Not so well." I took a sip from my mug, let Glory's brew warm my system.

"Have you been eating?"

"Yes."

There was a silence. I could imagine Chloe pondering what to say next, toeing the imaginary line that had formed a Tolkienian, Rowlingesque circle around me of late.

"I'm fine, Chubs", I reassured her, "Aren't we all?"

No, no, you're not, you're really not, was her unspoken response.

Instead, gently, as if to a child, she said, "We all miss him, Rache. You mustn't think we don't", letting my use of her childhood nickname slide. "I'll be in around four. Where should I look for you?"

"I need to take the hat over to Aunt Ung's later, but I think I should be back here by then. I'm at Wiseys."

"Alright, Wiseys then."

I snapped the phone shut, sipping at the tea intermittently, leaning against the table, working my tired neck. Above my head hung our class photos from years gone by, each framed in dark wood. Through bangs, side parts, bad perms, Chloe and Olivia always stood smack in the middle of the middle row, where heads and shoulders tapered away from them to a lesser height on either side. In the back, Yun and I would always hover, seeming giants, ungainly in our length. Briefly, I remembered Olivia saying in her last call to me that she had something to tell me. I glanced again at the blank sheet of paper, wondering what Yun would have wanted to say in his own eulogy.

Cold northerly winds.

***

Every time I visited the Ungs, I started off feeling like I should be on my best behaviour as soon as I stepped on the porch. The heavy, dark wood door in front of me, every inch of it covered with intricate carvings, put me in my place. I remember the day I thought I saw a boat float down the little path that led to the vacant house next to ours. Startled, I stepped back from the window and then pressed my face against it again, my hands leaving sweaty palm marks on the glass. It turned out that it was an ornately carved door, not a boat, and there had been two workmen underneath carrying it and not the swells of a mysterious tide. Soon after this was installed and the hinges tweaked, the Ungs, a family with a thousand stories and even more endearing turns of the spirit, had moved in. Slightly to the side of the door hung a bronze bell on a braided cord, which sounded dully when I pulled on it. I cocked my ears to listen for strains of Aunt Ung's favourite opera music, but the house was still. After a moment, the door swung open slowly, Yun's mother standing by it.

"Rachel." She opened her arms out to me. "Dear!"

I stooped awkwardly to hug Aunt Ung, a good half foot shorter than me. The house was, as I had already ascertained, still, as I stepped into the little silk slippers she offered me, leaving my shoes outside. My feet hung off the ends as I padded after her down the hall, our feet making hushed shuffling noises as we moved through the house, passing through corridors and doorways that were alternately lit and then shadowed, lit and shadowed, throwing soft accents on Aunt Ung's graceful back. When Yun and I were young, we spent hours playing hide and seek throughout the house, moving silently and waiting to catch each other's breathing, mimicking the ninjas in Aunt Ung's stories. Aunt Ung led me through the living-room, past dark wood settees padded with silk cushions in shades of green, purple and orange; Buddhist carvings and mini statuettes adorned the walls; a mobile made of paper-thin white seashells hanging from the ceiling, made a charming tinkling sound, moved by an unnoticed draft. She led me to the Paper Room separated from the rest of the house by a paper-thin sliding door, just past the bowl-shelf. We sat at a low table, looking out through the glass doors at the old oak table standing in the backyard, now being gently massaged by the (still) light rain. The murky sea above us was indecipherable.

"*Lai*. Have some tea," Aunt Ung poured me a small cup of tea from a grey and blue etched teapot on the table, as I crossed my long legs under me, "I feel the cold in my bones today."

We looked at each other, teacups in hand, across the few weeks that had broken our lives in two. The shift was from impossible to inevitable to the eventual setting of a new landscape, a haemorrhaging reality that defied the wisdom in her long dark eyes or the years writ lightly on either side of their lips.

I recalled the lone light in their house, this morning.

"Your mother called, she will not be here tomorrow." Aunt Ung sighed, shaking her head. "How much lighter our hearts, if your mother was here. Seems not so long since they left."

No words. She smiled at me sadly.

"Oh here, I brought the hat", I said, passing her a big, flat hatbox. The box was orange, with a black trim. Thanking me, she put it on the floor, lifting the lid just to peek inside. But that was all. She replaced the lid and slid the hatbox away from her, like she didn't want to talk about it yet.

"Rachel dear, have you had lunch yet?" she asked me, she who was always trying to feed me.

I shook my head no.

"You must eat," Aunt Ung said firmly, despite my feeble protests. I followed her through the door, but then gave up as I watched her disappear down the hall-way, her heavy masses of black hair twisted into a bun at the nape of her neck. Turning back, left alone amongst their things, he was inevitably everywhere; I cast about, averting my eyes until I caught my reflection in the gleaming surface of the black lacquer bowl-shelf.

The Ungs had a collection of bronze bowls, old hand-wrought bowls from all over Asia, bronze bowls tinged with a hint of green. According to Yun, the bowls were something of a family legacy, passed down through the generations as the collection grew. I remember days when the bowls would be all laid out, like washing on a laundry line, cleaned and then rearranged in a different order, Cappuccilli filling the air with his baritone Figaro. "*Ting zhe*", Aunt Ung would sometimes admonish us. Yun and I would cock our heads and look up at his mother, waiting for a lull in the music. She used to wear her hair higher, revealing the stiff collars of the cheongsams she loved to wear. Except on bowl-cleaning day of course. Wrapped in a silk dressing gown, she would stand with a small spoon in one hand, a bronze bowl in the other, the smell of jasmines caught up in the silk.

"Now listen again." And she would tap that bowl, issuing a clear, rounded peal. We would hold our breaths and listen into the perfect silence that followed.

"That is the most beautiful sound you will ever hear", she told us, bending down and leaning close into our faces, "Anywhere".

Without fail, that trick would keep us quiet for a precious few moments, seeking that most beautiful sound. I ran my hand along the rims of the bowls, feeling a sudden rush of Verdi, the smell of polish and laughter, wringing my soul out. I withdrew my hand. The connection lingered.

Half an hour later, I was sitting in the same place, a bowl of Aunt Ung's homemade noodles, *mien tiao*, in front of me. The *mien* were thin and white in a light chicken broth, topped with a small serving of minced pork, spring onion and some slices of preserved plum. My favourite noodles for as long as I could remember.

"Eat, eat!" Aunt Ung urged me. So I did. Across from me, she snipped at the ends of a huge mound of long pea-pods in preparation for Yun's wake, tossing the neat peas into a large, wide basket. I noticed that the calligraphy scrolls normally laid out were rolled up and stored at the end of the room. I guessed she hadn't been teaching lately.

"It's difficult."

Aunt Ung had been following my eyes, noticing my inactivity in the face of my noodles.

"How difficult to teach, to focus. And since this rain, I stored the scrolls, to prevent humidity." She gestured, barely audible, "I think only of my sons. Yun. Ang. There is little else." On her lips, his name was soft, the "*g*" almost silent, the "*u*" rounded. A fleeting image of a leather jacket and a warm, easy chuckle. She put the scissors and peapods in her lap, her head turned away for a fraction.

"Perhaps you may think this foolish." Her words were brave and tremulous, like a diver jumping through the air and slicing into the water. Looking back at me, I saw something unfamiliar in her eyes. I asked her what she meant, leaning forward, unsure if I really wanted to know, yet compelled by an awkward horrible forward momentum. For a moment, it looked like she was going to say more but she then shook her head. She resumed snipping off the ends of the pea-pods in quiet determination and I felt so very sorry that it wasn't my mother who sat in my place right now. We sat for a while longer, Aunt Ung trimming away at the peas, myself eating the noodles quietly. Maybe it was something she had not said, or it might have been the aroma of the chicken broth, inexplicably I felt the heaviness in my chest drop into my stomach and a chill run through my body. I blinked rapidly and cleared my throat.

"*Ba.*"

It was Uncle Ung. He stood at the sliding door, one foot across the threshold, looking at us.

"Ba", Aunt Ung said again, smoothing the mat next to hers, motioning for him to come in.

"Hi, Uncle Ung." I had not seen Uncle Ung since the hospital.

He nodded at me gently and then came in, crossed the room to sit near the glass doors opening out onto the backyard. His body was half turned away from us, facing the doors. He pushed open the glass sliding doors just a crack. The pitter-patter of rain trickled through, tainting our quiet. Aunt Ung spoke to him softly and he nodded. She got up and left the room again, leaving just the two of us and the sound of the rain. Unsure of whether I should speak to him, I sipped at my tea. In contrast to Aunt Ung, his hair was completely white, had been for as long as I could remember, combed back to reveal a high forehead. He wore a maroon vest over a white shirt and his shoulders seemed more hunched since I had last seen him. I thought of the tremendous energy that Uncle Ung had always exuded. We used to talk late into the night, and he, fuelled by endless cups of sake, would describe to us a scene, a moment in time, a turned silhouette, jumping to his feet to illustrate a point, slapping his thigh with a roar of laughter. But that was a long time ago.

"*Lai.*"

Aunt Ung had returned with a bowl on a tray. She knelt to place the bowl on the low table. The bowl held a soup of *tofu* and cured ham. Uncle Ung turned and started to drink it. The two of us ate to the sound of snipping and pitter-patter. Then with a final slurp, Uncle Ung finished. He thanked Aunt Ung and turned back to the window. Aunt Ung glanced at him, worry between her eyebrows. Finishing my last strand of noodles, I decided it was time to go. Announcing my departure, I shifted over to her side of the table to give her another hug. I could feel Aunt Ung wrap her arms around me in bone crunching desperation, briefly, before letting go and then smiling the same sad smile.

"Whatever may happen", she said quietly, close to my ear. I pulled back, a little afraid now but again she shook her head.

"We meet tomorrow", she said, squeezing my hands, "Thank you. Thank your mother for this most beautiful hat."

I nodded automatically. Getting to my feet, I felt the blood rushing through my legs as I said goodbye to Uncle Ung. Massaging them as I walked through the sliding door, I thought I saw in his reflection his shoulders rack with emotion, but then I blinked and I could have imagined it all.

***

The wind picked up the chimes and then let them fall against each other one by one. The door closed behind a man in a damp brown jacket leaving the shop empty-handed. I sat down at the counter, staring at the blank notepad in front of me. Nathan Brooks, the business card with the words CALL ME printed across it, screamed up at me. I picked it up, opened the desk drawer, dropped it in where it joined the other Nathan Brooks, and shut the drawer smartly. I would not CALL HIM. There was nothing to say. Back to my blank notepad. Then ten manicured fingers connected to two hands were flat on the desk right under my nose. Chloe. Overnight bag on the counter, overcoat draped over the overnight bag.

"Why are you staring at a blank piece of paper?"

"It's meant to morph into Yun's eulogy."

"Morph?"

"Yes."

"I see."

Chloe came round to my side of the counter, tumbling into the squishy armchair.

"This armchair needs re-stuffing", she said, shifting her weight and crossing her legs, her knee-high boots making a sound as they passed by each other. Her perfectly blow-dried shoulder length blonde hair shone in the light. She bent to begin unzipping her boots.

"Do you want something warm to drink?" I asked.

"I can wait till dinner", Chloe said. She laid out a few tissues and put her boots on them to keep the water off the carpet. I looked at my converse tossed carelessly in the corner, guilty. Finally settled, Chloe paused a moment, looking at me. Then she reached over and gave me a hug. All in due course.

I sensed a lecture I was not ready for on the tip of her tongue, so I jokingly remarked that I must look terrible. Chloe agreed, always having been nothing but straightforward with me. I turned away, tired already, deciding I could do with something warm to drink myself. Behind me, in her stockinged feet, Chloe might have struggled momentarily before deciding to leave the talk for later. She offered help with the eulogy.

"Well, I'm not sure how you could help", I answered, filling up a kettle. "I don't know where to start, mainly. That appears to be the problem."

She pounded on the side of the armchair.

"No use", I said warily, plugging the kettle in and flipping the switch. I turned back round to face Chloe.

Yun had not given dying a great deal of thought. He used to read through obituaries and laugh.

You can start with a list, Chloe remarked, I find that quite helpful.

A List?

Yes.

A List of What?

The wonderful things that made Yun. You might want to leave out the bad things though.

A gust that came in with the opening of doors disturbed the wind-chimes, and a woman's head poked round the side. Years of training compelled me loudly to offer assistance.

"Hi there, I was just wondering if you were holding story-book hour today?" At the woman's knees, a second head poked round the door, a mass of curly brown ringlets, rustle and squelch of Wellington boots.

I looked at her blankly.

"I know it's been cancelled a few times", the woman carried on a little uncertainly. "But I couldn't help but notice you were finally open."

I blinked.

"Rachel?" Chloe nudged me.

"I don't mean to presume, but if not, Mandy will be terribly disappointed." The woman's hands were on the little girl's shoulders. Mandy squelched.

"I...well...", I floundered. But Chloe stepped in.

"Yes, quite right, of course. Story-book hour will go ahead. At around four", Chloe said smoothly. "If you want to browse while you're waiting . . . or come back around then . . .."

"We'll come back, I'm just going to tell the others in Mandy's playgroup", the woman said gratefully. "See you later."

The door closed again.

Upon her departure, Chloe pulled on the edges of her skirt and looked at me pointedly.

"Why did you say yes?" I exclaimed, dismayed. "I don't have anything prepared."

"You have to. The kids have obviously been missing it", Chloe hissed, wiping her hands clean of the affair.

"No, you don't understand. I can't tell stories. Yun always did it."

Standing up, I raced over to the children's section, suddenly anxious, running my fingers along the multicoloured book spines. Behind me she probably rolled her eyes.

"I can't do it," I repeated, pulling out a *Magic Mice* book, "How about *Magic Mighty*?"

Chloe, by nature quick and always a little suspicious, folded her arms, "Why are you asking me?"

"Because you have to do it", I told her, tossing her the book and turning back to the shelf, looking for another.

"Rachel, I'm a journalist. I don't . . ." – the correct words escaped her as she leafed through *Magic Mighty* – " . . . entertain children."

"How about *Sarah Sailor's Excellent Adventure*?"

Chloe raised a perfectly arched eyebrow at me.

"You have to, really, you have to. Please. I would bore the kids to death", I implored.

On this point, Chloe had to concede. Relenting in disgust, she took *Sarah Sailor* from me.

"Fine, but only because I don't want the children to suffer." She cleared her throat experimentally. "That's something you can put in his eulogy."

"What?"

"That he was one hell of a story-teller."

***

"BOOM!"

Yun falls backwards off his stool, arms and legs splayed. The kids at his feet burst out laughing, and the adults chaperoning all smile in spite of themselves.

"After the dust had settled, Dr Google found himself buried beneath the rubble of his laboratory", Yun says, his voice muffled, coming from somewhere near the floor. "Something had gone wrong. Horribly wrong. He could feel it in his bones. He could feel it in his stomach. He could feel it in his . . ." – Here, a giant paw shoots up in the air; the little boy sitting in the front row says, CAT, loudly. –

" . . . whiskers!"

Yun emerges from behind the stool, wearing furry ears, a black nose with whiskers and holding a giant paw in each hand. The children burst into appreciative applause and laughter.

"He reached out a hand to brush dust off his face when his fingers felt the fur. Something had indeed gone horribly wrong, Dr Google thought to himself wildly. What would he tell his family? Would they make him sleep in the cat basket?" The same little boy clapped his hands excitedly, CAT BASKET!

Yun takes both fake paws in one hand and with the other, scoops the delighted little boy to perch on his knee. The child waves at his parents.

"Another thought occurred to Dr Google, a slow, scary, bone-chilling thought." Yun turns his serious eyes to the little boy then presses his ear to the boy's bellybutton, nose twitching. He looks back up at the child, shaking his head, and sets him back down into the crowd.

"What if his family didn't recognize him? Who would believe him now?" The children give a collective gasp and Yun signals to me with a wave of one paw. Holding up a bell, I ring it loudly.

"Sorry boys and girls, our story-teller needs a rest", I say over their groans, "You'll have to come back next week if you want to find out what happens to Dr Google."

Yun tumbles backwards off his stool again, one big paw waving goodbye to the kids. One by one, the parents come forward, bundling their kids away as they try to engulf Yun in a mini-tidal wave.

"Can I get the Dr Google series here?" a harassed looking father asks me, one eye on his kid in the reading pit, the other on me.

"Yes, of course. Would you like that now?" I answer, pleased.

"Yes, I'll take it. I really ought to take a leaf out of this young man's book – what's his name?"

"Yun. Yun Ung", I smile.

"My son won't go to bed at night, he keeps wanting to listen to the Dr Google stories again. But somehow, I don't quite have the knack." The father mimes a cat pawing at the air a little awkwardly. I stifle a laugh.

"Let me find you that box-set." As I make my way to the children's section, the father goes over to try to persuade his little boy to leave, without much success.

"You must be exhausted", I laugh, after I'd sent the little boy and father off with a huge package.

"These ears itch", Yun complains, loping towards the counter and removing the headband.

I pick up the ears, examining the teeth on the underside.

"Mm . . . I wonder if mum has something to fix this", I wonder aloud thoughtfully.

"There'd better be. I have at least two more hours of this Dr Google series."

Yun, hair now standing up on end in a way that strangely suits him, tosses the plastic nose and paws back into the black sports bag he carries costume parts in. He looks strangely preoccupied as he wanders back and forth in front of the table, trailing the tips of his fingers along the surface. He ambles over to the magazine rack, scanning the titles before picking up a snow-boarding magazine and flipping through it absently.

"Can't wait to go snow-boarding. Look at this guy, look at those tricks." His voice seems oddly flat all of a sudden and his expression has a pensive turn to it. I regard him, slightly bemused. So unlike him is this expression that I need a moment to recognize him wearing it.

"Can I get a drink?" He finally asks, setting the magazine aside.

"Yeah sure. Tea? I've got some nice stuff from Glory."

Turning my back on him, I pick up the kettle and start searching for the tea.

"How long have I been doing this for?"

"Doing what?"

"Story-book hour. How long have I been back?"

"I don't know. A year, maybe more. You didn't start helping me here straight away though."

"It seems like it's been less than that."

"Time flies when you're having fun", I quip.

"I was just thinking about the apartment I was staying in with George before I came back. It had one of those leaky taps that wouldn't stop dripping. It would wake me up at night."

"I hate those."

"I got up one night to tighten the damn thing and I slipped. Hit my head on the kitchen floor, I remember seeing those black and white tiles close up before I passed out. Next thing I know, I'm in the hospital and George is ringing mum and dad. One month later, I'm home."

I put my head to one side, thinking what a strange story to tell. "You never told me that story before." And I thought I knew them all. I should have known them all.

"Rache, I'm dying", Yun says from behind me. "So I won't be able to keep on doing the story-book hour indefinitely. You'll need to find someone else."

A Painted Moment

"Funny. That's a poor excuse for bailing on me", I say lightly, turning on the tap, "Where am I going to find someone else?" Except for the sound of running water, there is silence.
"Are you getting too busy at the hospice?" I ask, waiting for the kettle to fill, "I know you've been working really hard."
Is it possible for silence to grow or for icicles to crackle in the air? There is always a moment, when what was, is no longer, and what will come is no longer clear. This is my moment.
Abruptly, I swing around, kettle from the water splashing onto the floor.
"Yun? What did you say?"
Yun comes round the side of the counter, hands in his pockets.
"I said, I'm sick Rachel", Yun said calmly. Then, "Why don't you turn off the tap?"
"Oh." Splashing more water, I whip round and twist the faucet handle. Slowly this time, I turn again. Taking a few steps forward, I look at him uncertainly. He doesn't blink.
"I don't...what do you mean?"
Spreading his hands, Yun opens his mouth to speak, decides against it and instead takes the kettle from me and put it down on a side-table. Plugging it in, he flips the switch and returns to his perch leaning against the counter.
"I'm sick", he repeats simply, so characteristic.
My heart squeezes painfully. What do you mean, you're sick? I press on. Sick with a capital "S".
"What do you mean, though? You're sick?"
Yun heaves a sigh, searching for words. And I wait, dizzy on a precipice, cold sweat gathering on my forehead.
"I've known for a while, Rache, so it's not out of the blue or anything", he says carefully, "I'm dying. Nothing is going to happen today or tomorrow. But it's going to be sooner rather than later", he adds, his fingers digging through his hair again. "So I thought I'd better tell you."
Frost spreads through my chest like spider veins, choking my air.
"Why didn't you say anything about it before? Why didn't you tell me before?"
"I didn't think . . ."

"Why didn't you tell me before?!"
Yun looks away.
"What is it?"
He waves a hand, dismissing the question.
"I asked you. What is it?"
Yun sighs again.
"It's here", he answers briefly. "A thing. In my heart. Round about here", he points.
"But you're young. Surely someone can do something about it! You're only twenty-six." I am so shrill, a desperate, irrationally analytical, whirling, falling, reeling version of my self.
"It's not an age thing. They tell me I may have been born with it."
"So you've had it for years. You could be fine. Maybe you just need to rest." I reach out to grab his arm, shake it hard, "How can you be so sure?"
I am fierce. So very fierce. He and I, we are neither one of us ourselves at this moment, across from each other. I have not been as fierce since.
"I'm sure", he says. "There was a time when I wasn't, but that time has passed now."
What time? I wonder, as my world falls away. How long has he known, carried the burden inside him?
"Have you told anyone?"
"My parents. You." Yun pauses. "Ang."
Yun is quiet after that. His hands are back in his pockets and he looks at the floor. He is wearing his trademark long-sleeved tee and jeans. He is so lank and thin. The switch on the kettle bounces back noisily. Yun busies himself pouring out two cups of hot tea mixed with a dash of honey as I sink down into the armchair, a hand over my eyes.

A stone plummets to the bottom of a pond. We dance barefoot on the grass at the full moon. It always makes you do crazy things.

Yun passes me one of the mugs then sits himself on the multicoloured rug at my feet. We both try to sip at the scalding tea.

A Painted Moment

Finally.

"How long is sooner?" Is that my voice?

Yun puts his head on my knee, his face turned away from me.

"I don't know, six months. A year. Two." Later, one of us will question if it matters.

I stroke the back of his head. The tears will come later.

"It's not that bad, Rache." His voice is almost dream-like. "I just wanted to tell you, so you could start looking for another story-teller sometime soon."

***

Cold spaghetti-os eaten with chopsticks. Gabriel Garcia Marquez. Two bowls of rice, two bowls of soup, always in that order. Head between the knees to think better. Short-sleeved tees washed to a flaxen cotton softness. Long-sleeved tees gone awry at the wrist. Walks in the rain. Snow-boarding. Whiskey winters. Shochu summers. Zhang Yi Mou. Radiohead. Ice cold Snapples. Eyes that followed conversations. Always something to lean on. Broken hearts. Long term lovers. Skinny ribcage. Comfortable shoulders. Orange Sky. The glass is always half full but all I really need is a shot of a sense of humour. Or love. D.H. Lawrence. Checkered pajama bottoms, not striped. The trumpet, not the sax. Of course. Indiana Jones and his hat but not so much Sean Connery. German Shepherds. Re-runs of *Drunken Master* at one in the morning. One set of keys hidden in an old left boot. One set of keys on someone else's key chain. Unreturned letters to brother.

Chloe, of course, made an immaculate Fairy Godmother. Although we failed to establish in the twenty minutes we had, why a Fairy Godmother would be involved in *Sarah Sailor's Excellent Adventure*, the tall, pointy hat was the only prop I had that Chloe would deign to put on her head. Once again, I had padded out the reading pit with ottomans and beanbags. Glory had risen to the occasion with two big platefuls of biscuits, one chocolate chip, and the other oatmeal raisin. The children settled down cozily, mutedly munching on biscuits and listening to Sarah Sailor's story of single-handed bravery. Watching from behind the counter, I looked down at my piece of paper. Yun really had been a good story-teller. I had never heeded his advice to look for someone to take his place. Judging from the high turnout, all the kids really missed him.

I picked up one of the biscuits Glory had set aside for me and bit into it.

"And even though Sarah Sailor's head was spinning from where the whale's tail had walloped her, she did her best to grab hold of the whale's tail", Chloe read, adding, "Small as Sarah Sailor was, she managed this, impressively."

The little girls in the group were transfixed, the next generation of feminists, I thought; leave it to Chloe to inspire them.

"With a great roar, the whale ceased its thrashing, turning its small eye as far back as it would go. 'Why are you hanging onto my tail?' the whale intoned in its deep ocean voice." – Chloe, to her credit, lowered her own voice gruffly. –

"'Because you're making the tides swell and the sea churn.' Sarah Sailor cried, her voice a little squeaky compared to the whale's, 'My parrot is soaking and cold and all the boats are flooding with water.'"

Ten minutes later, I was shaken from my thoughts by a burst of applause from the reading pit. Chloe was curtsying to her appreciative audience and I realized that we had arrived at the end of *Sarah Sailor's Excellent Adventure*. Unlike Yun, this rather imperious story-teller would suffer no sticky hugs, so the little band of listeners were quickly retrieved and whisked away.

"It's great to have the story-telling back again", said the woman who had come in earlier, as she hovered by the door. Mandy was clutching her mother's leg shyly.

"Yes, it has been a while", I replied a little breathlessly, kneeling down so I was closer to Mandy, I asked, "Did you like Sarah Sailor?"

Mandy nodded then hid her face behind her wild curly hair.

"Is this girl new? She looks familiar but I don't think we've attended any of her sessions before", the mother asked, hoisting Mandy up into the crook of her arm.

"Chloe? Yes she is new; you could say that."

"Well, we'll miss Yun, won't we Mandy?" She touched her daughter's button nose lightly, "We liked the Dr Google series."

Mandy blinked her big innocent eyes at me.

"No more Dr Google?" She asked.

My reply stuck in my throat as I tried to say something, but could only touch her on the cheek before mother and daughter walked out, waving cheerful goodbyes.

"You left your umbrella on the tram in this sort of weather?" Chloe said incredulously, eyeing the dark sky and worsening rain. I didn't say anything, turned the key in the lock and tested the door to make sure.

"Glory said ten minutes."

From beneath the little canopy, Chloe and I watched as puddles formed on the ground. She was holding her overnight bag tightly to her chest, not putting it down lest it get wet. The ends of my jeans were getting decidedly damp. Glory had phoned after the departure of the children, asking us if we wanted a lift. Despite Chloe's doubts about Glory's driving skills, we had agreed to wait for her to close the coffee shop.

"So what are you going to do about the eulogy?" Chloe asked me. I didn't know. Across the street from us, I saw Amherst wiping down the windows of his store. He waved to me. Chloe and I waved back.

"Is Amherst coming tomorrow?" Chloe asked me.

"I think so. He says Yun still has a copy of his Ray Charles", I answered.

Amherst was a jazz aficionado. He had dedicated his life to jazz appreciation and converting others to become jazz fans. He beckoned for us to go over, but Chloe shook her head and pointed to her watch. Amherst nodded in understanding and we watched him do a quick jig before disappearing back into his store. Amherst had that rare quality of never appearing to love and never appearing to hurt. So he was always affable and easy to be around, yet all these years, I seemed to know very little about him. How could that be? I wanted to ask Chloe that, but remembered something else.

"I keep forgetting to tell you, there's been this man who keeps telling me to sell Wiseys to him", I said abruptly.

"Really?"

"Yes, really", I mimicked Chloe's elongated "l" sound. "He keeps dropping off his business card, telling me to call him. Nathan Brooks."

"Brooks... that name is so familiar. Have I read about him before?"

"He's new to me."

"Brooks...Nathan Brooks...It'll come back to me. So, what do you make of his proposition?"

"Sell Wiseys?" I snorted.

"Yes, sell Wiseys."

I likened the idea to selling my own blood, Chloe's eyebrow rising at my dramatic response.

"Did he make you an offer?" She asked matter-of-factly.

"Mr Brooks? No, he didn't. All he said was that he loves the store and he would come back with a proper proposal", I answered, pulling my coat in a little closer and brushing a strand of hair out of my face. For no real reason, I was uncomfortable with the topic, so I decided to change it.

"I'm sorry Chubs I haven't been reading your column lately. What've you been writing about?"

Chloe paused at the sudden change in the topic of conversation and I watched as several mixed expressions played across her face like clouds racing over a clear blue lake.

"That's ok. I haven't been writing well anyway," Her voice seemed strangely muted, "I've been quite distracted. Careless." She shifted her overnight bag, then looked across the road at Amherst's store.

"You'll be back on form in a while", I said automatically.

She twitched, burying her nose in her bag and then looking at me, resigned.

"I'm going to tell you something but you have to promise not to bug me about it."
I can't promise.
"Would you rather not know?"
"No."
"Well then, the paper fired me about a week ago", she said finally, her voice flat.
I thought I had misheard, incredulity escaping me almost as soon as the words registered.
"You heard me", Chloe repeated.
"That's not possible. Last week?" I gasped.
She nodded.
Momentarily, I was at a loss for words. What would they replace her column with? I had always been under the impression that Chloe was the paper's brightest star, a hard path to climb in the city but she had achieved it. It must have been the best thing to happen to her since she'd left school.
"I know. It was the best thing to ever happen to me."
That's not what I was going to say.
"How did it happen? They loved you."
Chloe tossed her perfect hair, didn't say anything.
"Chubs? What happened? Why didn't you say anything earlier?" I asked again, quietly. I touched her shoulder. She did not usually like being touched when she was upset.
"I didn't feel like it, I was worried about you", she answered back, shaking me off and shooting me a bright smile, "I'll be fine."
"Chubs."
"Don't call me that! Now shush, no more questions", she reminded me. "Oh look, here's Glory!"
Sure enough, Glory had pulled up in front of Wiseys in her small golf cart. She waved at us, motioned us to get in as she bent down to un-tack the flaps pinned to each side of the compact vehicle. Chloe blithely hurried round to the other side of the car, her arm raised against the rain. I climbed in on my side and re-tacked the flaps tightly to stop the rain getting in.
"Hey Chloe", Glory smiled.

Chloe stashed her bag in the back next to a pot of juniper, before turning and giving Glory's shoulder a squeeze.

"Hi, I haven't seen you in ages! Is Josh coming on his own?"

"Yeah, he's driving the other car. We should get going, otherwise he'll beat us." Glory backed the golfie onto the main road.

Together in the back, I looked at Chloe again, who refused to meet my eye.

"So how are things in the city?" Glory asked, looking at us in the rearview mirror.

"Good, you know, it's the city", Chloe replied, "Crazy, always crazy."

I thought about the day when I heard she got the job. I was carrying a stack of books that I dropped when the phone rang. I didn't reach the phone the first time, so she had to call back.

"It's me! I got it!"

Horns were blaring in the background and the connection was horrible.

"What?"

"I said I got it! The column! The job!" Chloe was almost screaming.

"The column? That's fantastic!"

"I had to pull sick leave to get out of the office to come over here and sign. No more pointless magazine articles! This is the real deal."

"Congratulations, Chubs, I am so proud of you."

"They even gave me a lap-top! Isn't that great?!"

"What will you be writing about?"

"Anything and everything. Life in the city. Being young and free. I must be dreaming. When are you coming here to celebrate with me?" She was, rightfully, beside herself.

"It might be a week or so before I get the chance, Chloe. A new set of books just came in – " She cut me off.

"Forget it, I'm getting on the next ferry back. Tell Yun. I want a bottle of his best shochu!"

We were up all night by the water. There was not one bottle of shochu, but two. A magnum of champagne. A purple and yellow checked blanket. The salty smell of clean seawater. Some nights are remembered for their beauty, some for their liberty, some others like this night, we remembered for its clarity and pitch. Three years ago. It was uncharacteristic of Chloe to keep something like this to herself. And so, yes, I was shocked but I was also hurt.

"I loved your piece last month. It was hilarious!" Glory was saying.

"That's me, funny", Chloe answered, absently.

Through the golfie's windscreen wipers, I saw we had reached the waterfront, Glory slowing down as we approached the restaurant, looking for a parking space nearer the entrance, Chloe twisting to point out spaces and Glory rejecting them if they were too tight. Hopping out, Chloe and I huddled under an umbrella as Glory fastened down the flaps securely against the rain. We ran for the large terrace, where during better weather the owner would pull back the green and white canopy and light the large hurricane lamps set along the floor. Tonight though, there was only one couple sitting bravely under the canopy, which bore the brunt of the rain. Pushing through the large glass doors, the sound of the rain faded into the background of glasses clinking, knives scraping dishes and warm laughter. We hung our coats on the coat-racks and stuck our umbrellas into a serviceable bucket by the door. Chloe spotted our table; she led the way, her blonde hair shining in the light, to a table for eight, right next to the fireplace at the centre of the restaurant where Glory's husband, Josh, Sylvain and James Aimes reigned. They had the air of boys caught in the act of slightly naughty behaviour, exchanging embarrassed glances, their conversation guillotined too cleanly. The bigger of the two other men stood up to greet Chloe in the beginnings of a hug but was rebuffed when she kissed him nonchalantly on either cheek, murmuring Hello Syl, her hands firmly on his forearms, her decision to do just that made in the short time it took to cross the restaurant floor. She then reached past him to greet the other – James Aimes in the same way, quickly debasing Sylvain's significance in the group. Glory had already taken the seat next to Josh without fanfare, leaving me an understudy to a grand stage act, unbalanced, about to greet

Sylvain whom I had known for more than fifteen years, like an awkward stranger.

"Hi Rache, you look good", Sylvain said leaning into me in what was half a hug and half a hearty pat on the back.

"Thanks, thanks," I answered, almost gushing, hearing it in my voice and hating myself for it, "As do you." He looked more than a little uncomfortable, still in his shirt, tie hanging lazily undone.

"Sit, sit", he gestured, unnecessarily taking on the role of host. I took the seat opposite Josh, Chloe to my right, an empty chair to my left across from Sylvain. Presiding over the discreet chair scrapings, adjustments to hair, clearing of throats, was the loud sound of appraisal. In our initial silence, Josh asked too loudly if we were expecting eight people, before Glory reminded him Olivia had yet to arrive. Sylvain nodded. He seemed tired as he picked up his beer glass in an attitude that struck me as oddly adult, just shy of sloppy. I turned to Chloe who had lapsed quickly into conversation with James Aimes at the end of the table, one hand held out to catch the waiter's attention, the other rested lightly next to James Aimes'. I looked back at Sylvain, whose eyes had followed mine. He shook his head almost imperceptibly.

"Same old weather", Sylvain said finally, trying to focus on what was ahead of him.

"I hope it lets up tomorrow", Glory said anxiously. Josh patted her on the arm reassuringly.

"So Rache, how long has it been since I last saw you?" Sylvain asked, "Two, perhaps three years?"

"I think so", I answered vaguely.

Glory asked if it had been when Sylvain's mother had had a boating accident (Sylvain and Josh trying to date Josh's visits over the last few years).

As Sylvain talked, his eyes kept flickering towards Chloe, as if drawn by her golden hair. Briefly, it crossed my mind that there were people who ran away from this place, each with their tail between their legs, chasing it round and round in circles. There seemed something different, something inexplicable and intangible that I couldn't put my finger on. Sylvain pulled on the knot of his tie again, clearing his throat like it was still tight against his adam's apple. He caught me watching him and frowned slightly. Sylvain looked bigger – had always been quite big in his easy six foot two inch frame – but his shoulders filled out his suit more now and he seemed to have the beginnings of a beer gut.

"So", he hedged, compelled to speak now that I had caught his eye.

"Yeah", I nodded, straightening my place-mat compulsively, "So. How's work?"

"Good, good – I mean no, it's hell but it's – " Sylvain seemed to panic and then instinctively relax in the comfort of talking about a safe topic, "Work is work y'know. I – yeah". He fell silent again, perhaps hearing his own voice, too abrasive.

"What are you doing now?" I asked, even though I knew the answer.

"Banking." His voice assumed a slightly modest tone as if to emphasise it wasn't an achievement.

"What you've always wanted to do, right bro?" Josh clapped him chummily on the shoulder. Sylvain looked embarrassed for a moment and I suddenly recalled that it wasn't what he'd always wanted to do at all. Sylvain's father was a banker who had always wanted his son to follow in his footsteps but Sylvain had never shown any real inclination. Josh was looking at us expectantly now, his hand still on Sylvain's shoulder.

"Which bank do you work for?" Glory asked, oblivious, on the other side of Josh.

"J.P Morgan", Sylvain said quickly.

"Is that the one Terry Reed works for?" Glory asked Josh.

"Terry who?"

"Terry Reed, from the year above us?"

Josh shrugged.

"I think she works for Morgan Stanley", Sylvain answered.

"Yeah, yeah, one of those", Josh jumped in animated for another moment.

We fell silent again. At the other end of the table, James Aimes' voice could be heard clearly.

"Who's singing bad karaoke? That you, Aimes?" Sylvain's voice rose, his chest puffing a little.

"Me, my clients, everyone," James Aimes said expansively and Sylvain chortled, "Who knew karaoke could be this bad?"

"Why do you have to go with them?" Chloe asked, her nose wrinkling derisively.

"The leisure of a famous pen does not belong to me," James Aimes sighed, "You will never know what it's like to be a sales guy."

Chloe fell silent.

"What is it you sell now, Aimes?" Glory asked.

James Aimes' head snapped in Glory's direction; he had always had a side parting and his slightly wavy hair flopped towards her.

"A press distribution service", he said vaguely, but adding significantly, "We're global."

"Right," Josh nodded a beer at him, "Right." The lack of interest settled like foam on a cheap drink.

Chloe glanced at Josh sharply, perhaps surprised at his dismissive agreement, but Glory asked the question for him, only in earnest, and listened, her eyes gradually glazing over as James Aimes launched into a longish speech about the computer system that his company had helped develop. While James Aimes talked, Chloe asked a hovering waiter for menus. The waiter doled them out and told us that the special of the day was orange roughy on a bed of mashed parsnips, Glory asked if we should wait for Olivia. I didn't have to look up from the menu to know what expression Chloe would be wearing.

"What are you having?" Chloe asked me as if she hadn't heard Glory.

I wasn't that hungry.

"You should eat more," Chloe said absently perusing the menu, "Have some soup and some mussels or something. You can have some of my crab."

Across from me, Glory battled indecision between the special of the day, roughy, and steamed cod. James Aimes wondered aloud if he was still allergic to shellfish, Sylvain wordlessly plunked his beer glass down on the table, rattling the other glasses standing empty along it. Our waiter returned to take our orders, twice taking Glory's who finally settled on the seafood tagliatelle.

"I heard that Germaine Bond is getting married next year", James Aimes announced with a sneer as the waiter scurried away.

"Germaine Bond?" Chloe asked incredulous and wide eyed.

"Did she get knocked up?" Sylvain asked.

"Really, is that quite necessary?" Chloe tossed impatiently at Sylvain who held up his hands in mock compliance.

"Who else is getting married?" Glory asked the table at large.

I arranged my face into a mildly interested expression and found my attention drifting, unable to feel excitement at the imminent matrimony of our friends from high school who had, most of them, never been that close in the first place. Perhaps a sign of age, what used to matter, albeit slightly, barely registered on the emotional richter scale now. Josh and Sylvain launched into a slightly tortuous conversation about cars while Chloe and Glory picked at the topic of marriage. My head ached. Our conversation had never seemed so trivial.

"Rache?"

Chloe's big eyes searching my face told me that my input was required. Patiently, she repeated herself.

"Do you remember Bill Watson?"

I furrowed my brow in concentration.

"William Watson?" I was quite sure that no one by that name had ever existed.

"Big Bill? Guy with glasses?" James Aimes motioned with his hands, indicating exactly how big Bill had really been.

"What about him?"

"I was just telling the girls, he's done really well for himself, he's into funding and selling start-ups, lives in a plush stack at the top of a hill."

"Seemingly against the odds", Chloe commented appraisingly.

"He's meant to have lost a lot of weight, still single though", James Aimes added with a slight smirk. The low light of the restaurant cast odd angles on our faces and James Aimes' nose appeared particularly beak-like, the right side of his face mostly in shadow, the other side flushed from perhaps too much beer.

Still trying to make sense of what the point of that little side story about William Watson was, I turned my head at the sound of a familiar voice. It was Olivia, striding over to the table in a flash of dark jeans and high boots, a large leather bag in one hand. A chorus of greetings rang out as she took the seat next to mine, stashing her bag on the floor and smiling around at everyone, reaching out to squeeze Glory's hand across the table. She turned to look at me, her face softening as she swept me into a fierce hug. I could smell her shampoo, the touch of ylang-ylang and the faintest trace of cigarettes. Feeling a lump at the back of my throat, I pulled away, blinking rapidly.

"Rachel." – Her long, smoky almond-shaped eyes narrowed in concern. – She put her hand to my cheek and then smiled, not saying anything. I smiled back. The waiter returned to our table, proffering a menu, straightening the napkin draped over his left arm. Olivia thanked him and for a moment the waiter stopped short, basking in the warmth of her attention. Then Olivia turned away, and he was left hanging. He quickly straightened and slunk away to a suitable distance, still within earshot but comfortably invisible.

"I feel like some piping hot clam chowder", Olivia said absently, looking through the menu, "And a tall glass of cold white wine would go down a treat".

"Hear, hear", Sylvain agreed, lifting his glass and peering through the empty bottom of it.

Olivia made her order with the waiter, causing him a mild heart attack by smiling at him and asking for more wine, then turned back to face the rest of the table. Glory squealed, grabbing Olivia's long slender hand and pulling her half way across the table, exclaiming over her rings. Josh put his head down on the table as Sylvain craned his neck curiously to see what was so special about the ruby and emerald gold rings on our friend's lovely fingers. The two gems were cut into slim rectangles and set into the gold rings in one smooth surface. Chloe had gone very still. I noticed how the rings caught the light.

"Where did he get them?" Glory asked.

"Istanbul. I think he picked them up at one of those traditional markets." Josh groaned. Olivia smiled diplomatically, taking her hand away and tucking a loose strand of hair behind her ear with the other.

"I'm sorry I'm late, anyway. I missed my ferry." Olivia beamed gently around the table at everyone. "So. It takes something like this for us all to be together again, then."

There was an awkward silence, as everyone tried to look elsewhere, nowhere, anywhere but at each other or at her, the glaring truth too much to stand up to. I see, she said. In our silence, the waiter came forward to pour more wine for everyone, the trickling sound accusingly loud amidst our stoppered utterances. Chloe had her arms crossed in front of her, staring straight ahead. Olivia drank experimentally from her wine glass and then removed a pack of cigarettes from her bag. With one elbow on the table, she put a cigarette to her lips and lit it elegantly, an image of Holly Golightly without the cigarette holder.

"Can I bum one?" James Aimes called from the other end of the table.

Olivia made a motion to pass the pack to him before Sylvain tossed his own pack through the air, making a grumbling comment about James Aimes and his inability ever to buy his own cigarettes.

"What are you doing now, Aimes?" Olivia asked.

Through his initial puff of smoke, his eyes narrowed, James Aimes sighed appreciatively.

"Sales. Press distribution." He had to add, "Global Press Distribution."

"Don't ask him what that means," Sylvain said, rubbing his eyes with the heels of his hands, "Otherwise, we'll be here all night talking about computer systems."

James Aimes scowled at him as Josh and Glory laughed nervously, perhaps unsure if his displeasure was genuine.

"And you, Syl, what do you do then?"

"Banking, J.P. Morgan", Sylvain said promptly.

"It's not the same bank where Terry Reed works", James Aimes interjected, showing that he knew.

Olivia raised pleasantly surprised eyebrows.

"And how is that?" Olivia had the habit of starting sentences as if she was right in the middle already, with few opening words, plunged almost right to the hilt from the start.

"Work is work," He said again, shrugging, non-committal.

"Right, it is isn't it?" She kept her voice light, her eyes trained on his face. And to his credit, Sylvain managed to hold it for a moment before sliding away. Where is it written that old friends remain friends for life?

"It isn't like it's a coffee shop unfortunately." Sylvain acknowledged Josh and Glory with a slight nod of the head.

"I assume that's going well."

"Well, quite well. I don't spend enough time there though, Glory's doing most of the work there these days it seems." Josh patted Glory on the hand again.

"Well, someone has to greet people with a smile in the mornings. You're better off doing all the wheeling and dealing with those truck drivers."

"She means vendors", Josh said. She gave him an affectionate punch on the arm.

"I miss your coffee, I've been around the world and I've never tasted better."

"Is that a song?"

"That reminds me, we have to stock up again, we're running low."

"What – I've been around the world?"

"Yeah. How does it go?"

"If it is a song, I've never heard it", Olivia laughed lightly.

"At least you've learnt to be punctual", Glory pointed out, getting back to Sylvain. "We didn't expect you to be here till tomorrow."

"Funny," Sylvain said deadpan, "How on earth do you expect me to be late for tomorrow?"

"What is the plan for tomorrow anyway?" James Aimes asked the group in general, pausing in his conversation with Chloe who was tearing at her bread, lips pressed together.

Everyone except Chloe turned to look at me expectantly. Taking a deep breath, I said deliberately, "We're all meant to be at the cemetery – the one over by the gorge – at two." I cleared my throat. "I'm going to be speaking – briefly. I think either Mr or Mrs Ung will also be speaking... and..."
I paused. No-one said anything.
"Then, we're all going over to the Ung's after, for the wake. Aunt Ung has been preparing for days now, so I know there's going to be a lot of food. I know there's going to be a lot of people there at any rate. Lots of relatives And I think that's it."
I came to a faltering end, hoping someone would jump in with a reliably bad joke. Sylvain picked up his glass to drink from it, realized it was empty and said wryly, "I think we all need another drink."
Olivia nodded in agreement.
"Where are you boys staying tonight?"
"I'm staying with these two", Sylvain nodded at James and Glory, while clinking his fork against his glass to get the attention of the waiter. I heard Chloe tut-tut under her breath.
"I'm staying with my parents", James Aimes said from the end of the table.
"And I'm the one with the full house of girls tonight", I commented.
"You could use the company", James said a little too seriously. Glory shushed him immediately, but not before another uncomfortable silence descended on the table. Cigarette butts smouldered in the ashtrays and I fancied I could hear the drop of ash.
Thankfully, all the food seemed to arrive at the same time, filling the strained air with the comforting smells of excellent cooking. Soon everyone was more occupied with devouring his or her entrées to say much. I prodded listlessly at my mussels. I had never thought of myself as wanting in company before Yun died. I wondered if that thought had also crossed his mind too, when he told me to look for another story-teller.
I tried to focus on my self, seeing an outline of my body and thinking, that's all, that's all it is.

A Painted Moment

"Your mussels no good?" Chloe asked.

I didn't say anything.

"Eat." She was pushing some of her crab onto my plate.

"I *am* eating", I protested.

"Eat", she said again.

Slowly, I broke apart the claw, digging out some of the steaming meat, the smell wafting up my nostrils. Sylvain cut vigorously at his fish, the detached decorative head trembling with his back and forth motion, eyes wobbling glassy and dull. A wave of pain numbed my brain again. The shiny scales were almost reflective, artificial and sinister in their collective need to break apart.

"While I'm here, you eat", Chloe said under her breath.

***

The rain had worsened.

"You mind telling me how we would have gotten home in your car?" Josh snorted, the mini creeping along the road, tires rolling noisily through puddles. He snorted again as he slowly manoeuvred a turn, his body hunched forward over the wheel.

"It's not that bad yet", Glory answered defensively, trying to peer through sheets of rain.

"Hey!" Sylvain said suddenly, sitting up quickly. "Which street are we on?"

"Cadogan", I answered. "We're coming up to Wiseys just ahead."

Sylvain pressed his forehead to the glass as our car went past.

"I haven't looked at Wiseys in years", Sylvain said finally. "It looks exactly the same. Is it the same?"

"It's exactly the same", I answered obligingly.

"The same, huh?" Sylvain said almost wistfully. In the dark, I nodded. Wiseys receded behind the car and he twisted back round in his seat regretfully.

"You know, if you're not that into your job now, you could really start thinking about what else you would rather be doing", Olivia said abruptly, back on their previous topic.

It took a moment for Sylvain to realize Olivia was talking to him. The nostalgic sight of Wiseys seemed to have confounded him. From within his cocoon of memories, he flailed.

"What?"

"If you don't like your job," Olivia repeated, "Banking."

"Quit banking? To do what?"

"How about travel?"

"Travel."

Olivia laughed, her hand going gently to his shoulder. Do you remember the careers project we had to do in Form Four? You brought this huge map in, wore these big trekking boots?

It was my turn to laugh.

Travel, then work, travel some more.

"That was years ago", Sylvain said absently, tracing circles on the car window.

"It's not too late to do something about it", Olivia said her face half hidden in the shadows.

"What about you? You haven't mentioned William at all this evening."

"Will is fine. In Florence. He's fine in Florence, on tour for his book. Writing." This, as if on autopilot.

"What do you do when he tours?"

"I travel with him", Olivia answered. "I get to see the place that way. A lot more than he does anyway. He's always got some engagement. Hopefully this year will be better. Quieter. I thought about going back to university."

"Traveling and studying. That sounds the life", Glory said from in front.

In the dark, Olivia's head turned just a fraction towards her as Josh cut in with talk about a new building that had sprung up near where Sylvain used to live.

Abruptly, Glory twisted around in her seat.

"How was story-book hour?" She asked.

I nodded, a thumb out at Chloe, "Our fairy godmother here was great," I answered. "The kids loved it."

Glory looked like she wanted to go on but she twisted back round. Feeling like I needed to do something, I patted the back of Glory's seat, "Thanks for the biscuits."

"No problem", she said. "You know I'd be happy to do that again. Supply biscuits. Next time." Her eyes flicked up to the corner of the rear-view mirror for an instant.

I made a noise of consent, looking out of the window, watching the wind and the rain whipping at the trees along the quiet streets. I thought vaguely about what Chloe had confessed today, wondered what she was thinking and how she was feeling this very moment listening to Olivia talk about her carefree lifestyle.

"We're almost there", I said quietly to Chloe. She had not said anything the entire journey, I'd assumed she had fallen asleep. Her eyelids fluttered open quickly.

"There should be an extra umbrella just under the seats", Josh said, coming to stop in front of my house. Sylvain reached down to fish one out and offered it to Chloe, who accepted it wordlessly. Saying our goodbyes, the three of us quickly jumped out of the car and skipped through puddles to the front door.

"Just leave the umbrella out here", I said, turning the key in the lock and sliding the doors open. The house was chill, but still warmer than outside.

I flicked on the light switches and light from the hanging lamps in the hall illuminated the rooms. I saw Choe's quick look of surprise at the white draped furniture as she shrugged off her overcoat and hung it delicately over a chair.

"Does anyone want a drink?" I called over my shoulder as I headed through the dining room to the kitchen, "I have a bottle of chianti open. Or something stronger if any of you wants."

In a side room at the back of the kitchen, I busied myself turning on the heating systems that would warm the house and our bath water. I found the bottle of wine and some glasses and walked back out into the dining-room to find the two of them sitting at the dining-table. Or rather Olivia was sitting and Chloe was half in and half out of her chair as if she hadn't quite made up her mind.

I looked at the two of them pointedly, then silently began pouring the wine. I had long ago given up reasoning with Chloe about Olivia. There was only so much I could do or say while still keeping Chloe as a friend.

"How is Aunt Ung?" Olivia asked me, more at ease, taking the glass I passed her.

"Keeping it together," I said honestly, handing Chloe hers, "Just barely. But still better than Uncle Ung. I haven't really spoken to him since – since the hospital."

"Have you seen him?" Chloe asked, her voice clipped.

"Today, briefly", I said, putting aside the bottle and gripping my glass, "When I took the hat to Aunt Ung."

"And?"

"And it was almost like I wasn't there," I answered.

The three of us contemplated this for a moment. I rubbed at the bridge of my nose.

"How are you?"

I looked up and realized Olivia was looking at Chloe intently.

"Fine, quite fine", Chloe answered coolly. "And you?" There were few things or people that Chloe allowed to fluster her, as a matter of principle. It was a reluctant follow-up question, a demonstration of the shift in power. Olivia smiled faintly, perhaps that thought had crossed her mind too.

"I've had better times", Olivia answered swiftly. I could see Chloe was caught off guard by her frankness. Even I was. Olivia, golden, tawny, graceful, Olivia had always led one of those lives where the soles of her feet barely touched the grime and grit of reality that became the lives that other people lead. Chloe didn't say anything, turned the glass in her hand. I began to reach out across the table.

"I'm pregnant", Olivia said matter of factly.

Her announcement, so unexpected, so foreign were those words that it was moments before I could grasp the meaning.

Pregnant?

The idea of Olivia as mother, though alien, appealed to me as she had always loved children. Then too quickly, I remembered the smell of cigarettes on her.

Chloe seemed in shock, speechless.

"How many months?" I blurted out, uncertain.

She held up two fingers as she lifted the wine glass to her lips, *supposed to keep it quiet still*. My first instinct was to reach out and hug her, but something in the way those two fingers struck the air told me this was not a moment to celebrate.

Unsure, I turned my attention back to Chloe who was like a statue coming back to life. She drained her glass, closed her mouth firmly and carefully set her jaw.

Congratulations.

She got up, retrieved her bag and walked off down the long hall towards the bed-rooms. The two of us watched her stiff back and raised head, her footsteps echoing in the hall until she closed the guest room door.

"Oli." Now I did reach out to touch her arm. "I can't believe it."

"Neither can she, apparently," she said bitterly. "Nothing changes."

She took another drink from her glass.

"I'm going outside for a smoke," Olivia told me, rifling through her bag for a pack and getting up, her chair scraping across the wooden floor.

I followed her through the glass doors of the kitchen out onto the porch, dimly lit by the kitchen lights. Everywhere were small pools of water attended by patterns of finer spray. She removed a cigarette and lit it, the end glowing orange in the half dark.

Shouldn't you not be smoking, I pointed out from behind her, just inside the doorway, crossing my arms against the cold.

Olivia regarded her cigarette thoughtfully.

Probably, she told me.

The rain came down, drawing long lines through the air and creating a fuzzy outline of the Ung's house in the distance. The air was cold and heavy with ozone.

I don't know if I want this baby. The words came to me a hollow echo, ephemeral. An image of Yun sprang to mind. We were eleven and he had just received his first valentine. Holding out a red paper heart, he was embarrassed. But I don't want it, he had said weakly.

I regarded Olivia, not sure what to say, afraid I might trespass on this whole new world of her and her baby, where I had yet to find my bearings, if indeed there were any to find. The smoke from the cigarette curled up and folded in a long thin stream.

"Why not?" I finally asked timidly, deciding that was safe.

She thought for a moment, leaning against one of the pillars that held up the porch roofing. For the first time, I noticed how tired she looked. I huddled into my sweater, wondering if she was cold. "I don't think it would be fair on the baby," she said carefully, "to bring it into a family that might not always be one."

"I might leave William", she said shortly.

"Leave William?" I parroted. Olivia exhaled deeply as she nodded.

"Might. I haven't made up my mind yet."

"But..."

Olivia merely nodded again.

"What's happened?" I added. "What's happened with you and William?"

She was quiet again, for the longest of times while nature unfolded around us, oblivious to whatever human drama we enacted in our stop-and-start silences and sympathies.

"Maybe I never really loved him."

"Don't say that."

"It's true. I've been wondering if I ever really loved him. Maybe it's been nothing more than flight and fancy, romance and poetry." She stopped to drag again on her cigarette. "His poetry."

"But you knew, you wouldn't have if you didn't love him," I insisted. "You knew how Chloe felt. You must have loved him." You don't give up a friend for someone who hasn't made a permanent incision into your heart.

Olivia shook her head, abashed – no – grave.

"You're right. Of course you're right." She paused again. "I just – I remember waking up one morning as Will was getting ready to meet his agent. We were in Munich, in a lovely hotel room with high ceilings and gold faucets on the marble bathroom tops. He got dressed and then came to give me a kiss on my forehead before he left. I lay there for the longest time, not sure what I would do that morning, that day. I ran a bubble bath, I had breakfast in bed, I walked around the old town and bought some red and yellow peonies from the market even though there was no vase to put them in. I went back to the hotel room and sat there, not knowing what I was doing, where I was heading. It was like watching a gold-fish in a bowl."

"Just like that?"

"Just like that." Olivia looked down at her rings.

"I'm twenty-seven, Rache. I feel like my life has been running ahead while my mind has been someplace else. I'm twenty-seven and I'm pregnant and I'm married to Will. But I'm not sure this is what I want. Isn't it funny?"

Ain't that the thing?

She smoked the last of her cigarette and held the smouldering end out in the rain. It went out with a hiss.

"Knowing what you want is never easy", I said finally. Olivia sighed.

You shouldn't not know just because it's hard to make up your mind.

From burning bright lights to will-o'-wisps in the dark.

"And this is what you wanted to talk to me about? When you called?"

Olivia nodded.

"And I wanted to hear your voice. You've never felt so far away since you've moved back."

I shrugged, not knowing how to respond.

"Why did you come back?" She changed the subject abruptly.

"Why not?"

"Because there might have been other things for you."

I shook my head.

"And?" Olivia raised an eyebrow.

"And nothing."

"And you're glad because otherwise you wouldn't have been here when Yun passed away."

I turned my head away. Others might have said something like that to be hurtful. Even Chloe. – But Olivia. – She said things like that to remind us we were human and really, at heart, very broken and altogether the same nuts and bolts.

"I didn't know before I came home."

"Fate, it's a funny thing."

"Did we establish we believed in fate?"

Olivia looked at me.

How else?

I had never thought about it that way before. What then, the other turn in the road, the other ending. What would it have been like to find out over the phone, miles away, without him to comfort me afterwards?

"Mother used to say that age helps put perspective on our actions, but what's the use of understanding what your actions were all about until after you've made them?" Olivia said, "Such bullshit."

I sucked in air. It would have been unbearable.

And then we were quiet because Olivia had finished her wine and shut the door on the conversation.

Later I passed by the guest room Chloe was staying in. The door was ajar and the bedside lamp was still on. I thought of what she had told me earlier and wondered if I should go in to speak to her. In those long moments outside her door, I almost did, once, maybe twice, reaching out for the doorknob, but hesitating still. I stayed there for a long time, the taste of apprehension in my mouth. Not too different from adrenaline. Like iron. Or salt. Or shattered pieces of glass.

A Painted Moment

Part Two
I dreamed in red

*There once was a little girl named Lan, who lived with her
parents up in the mountains, where winter comes early and
spring comes late. They were poor and Lan was lonely because
there was no one to play with. On a particularly bitter night, Lan
and her mother waited long before the hearth because Lan's
father was very late. Suddenly, the door to their small cottage
blew open with the force of a thousand gales of wind. Standing
framed in the doorway was her father and a stranger wrapped in
a dark cloak. The stranger had collapsed and Lan's father had
decided to take him home. Together, they carried the stranger
over by the fire, laid him down and covered him with a blanket.
At first he dozed fitfully but then he fell into a deep sleep, tended
by Lan's mother. In the morning, when Lan woke, she heard
noises coming from outside her room. Rushing out, she saw that
the stranger was up and well again, and sitting at their dining-
table eating breakfast with her parents. When the old man saw
her, he smiled at her and beckoned her to sit next to him. The two
fell into conversation, as Lan's parents went about their daily
tasks. She told him everything. When Lan had run out of things to
say to him, he leaned forward till his nose was just inches from
Lan's.*

*"I have a secret to share with you, Lan", he said softly, his eyes
twinkling. "But you must promise not to tell anyone. What would
you do, if you had a friend to play with all day long, who would
take care of you, be loyal to you, love you for as long as you
needed?"*

*Lan's face shone with excitement, and that was the only response
the stranger needed.*

*So the stranger gave Lan a kiss on her forehead, patted her hand,
creakily got up and left the cottage. Lan chased after him,
watched him hobble off down the mountain, his beard fluttering
in the wind. Where is the friend you promised me?! she wanted to
cry. As she turned to go back into the house though, her shadow
cast itself across the ground and then it waved at her. Surprised,*

Lan jumped back, but her shadow didn't move with her. Instead, her shadow kept waving and started to dance around like a monkey would. Now delighted, Lan stuck out her hand and her shadow reached out and held it; hand in hand, the two walked away. From that day onwards, Lan was no longer lonely, because she had her shadow to keep her company. Lan's parents were surprised at the sudden change in their daughter; when they returned at night from work, they would find Lan tucked into bed, content, and not starving for attention as was her wont. As wisdom taught them not to question welcome changes, they kept their own counsel. As time is accustomed to, the years flew by and the day came when Lan's father decided that she was old enough to go to find work at the village at the foot of the mountain. So it came to pass that Lan found herself waving goodbye to her parents as they drove off in their cart, a cloth bag slung over her shoulder containing several changes of clothes and some food. She turned, as was her practice, to speak to her shadow, when she realized that her shadow was no longer beside her.

The sky is leaking cotton-balls, tumbling and drifting. Fluffy snowflakes tumble and drift, blow sideways, and then frost the dark shingles of the temple roof, the upturned eaves spearing, spoiling their icy formations. There is a decisive cold wind. Faint traces of incense waft out through the doorway, enticing the faithful to walk up the stairs and enter. It's warmer standing close to Yun, so I make sure to follow in his footsteps, till he laughs and pulls off his wooly cap and jams it on my head. His hair is standing up now and so it's my turn to laugh. Aunt Ung looks at us and smiles, shaking her head, its ok to talk, but don't disturb the other visitors. Mum motions to me to zip up some more. Olivia laughs for the first time that day and Chloe nudges her with her elbow, but we're all excited and it's hard to suppress the rising sense of euphoria as our feet leave prints on the freshly minted snow, crunching into reality. I'm sleepy but happy that we're all here together. I had worried Olivia might not come, no one to drive her as her parents are away on business as usual.

A Painted Moment

Mum rose to the occasion to fetch her though, and the bag she's carrying over her shoulder contains clothes for a sleep-over tonight. I'm excited about that too. Uncle Ung, Dad and Ang are walking ahead, at the top of the stairs, disappearing through the first doorway of the temple. As I put one foot on the bottom step, I peer curiously at the quiet huddle of people around me, wrapped in thick coats, carrying bags of oranges, talking softly to each other, earnest in their endeavour this early morning, sure of their faith while we are only passers-by. Chloe, now at the top of the short flight of stairs, beckons to Olivia and me, Yun and Sylvain and we hurry to catch up with her. At the top of the stairs, we stop and look up. The grand entrance reaches up and away from the stone steps in a splendour of dark sandalwood, majestic, reassuring, graced on either side by faded red doors and a large plaque at the top. What does it say, I whisper. Peace for all generations, Yun whispers back. We stand for another moment, awed by the sentiment, he and I. Just through the door, a stone screen wall. We can't see beyond it, but we hear noises, so after another moment's hesitation, we move forward. Immediately, my foot catches on something and I fall forward with a sharp cry, but before I hit the ground, Yun and Sylvain grab me by the back of my parka and haul me up.

"Sorry, I forgot to tell you, you have to watch out for these *men lan*. You have to step over, one leg at a time, like this." Yun demonstrates, stepping respectfully across the raised threshold that is a burnt, crimson red. Different from the outer walls of the temple – the pointed, shingled roof and classical eaves – but the same shade as the pillars. We move around the screen wall, through to the forecourt and the words on my lips evaporate. In the middle of the forecourt, open to the sky, stands an ancient willow, its branches weighed down with snow, its roots just beginning to buckle the stone floor it's been set in. Under the small mounds of snow, I see faded colourful ribbons tied in knots, at their ends are small tags with indecipherable writing. Even its trunk is decorated, long seemingly endless lengths of string, red and white, wound around it. Small pieces of paper are folded a few times over and tucked in to the string. Almost without realizing, I approach and put my palm against its bark. Rachel! I turn. The others have moved to one side and Yun is calling me. What are these writings? Hopes. Whose hope? Everyone's. People write down their wishes and pray for them to come true. Wishes? Yes. We can come back and write some too.

The forecourt is edged on three sides by narrow corridors where small wooden doors seem to lead elsewhere. We make our way down one of them, Yun slightly ahead, showing us the way, the uninitiated, the inexperienced. The bitter cold of the morning is left behind as the smell of incense wafts out once again, but this time it is much more intense and there are clicking noises, a collected rhythmic beat that I've never heard before. We cross a second threshold to the very heart of the temple, the reason we've been invited by the Ungs to join them. At the centre of the room where the roof rises up, on a pedestal is a reclining figure of Buddha, surrounded by huge bronze urns of different sizes on all sides. All around us, people are lighting incense, kneeling on faded, almost threadbare brown cushions, palms together, fingers pointing upwards, clasping incense, praying; others are shaking things that look like pencil stands, only instead of pencils they contain long, thin reeds. Above our heads, huge incense coils spiral upwards, the ceiling is covered with them, each one giving off a heady smell and thin streams of white smoke. There is the inaudible hum of a centuries-old system of faith and belief. I ask Yun what the reeds are. *Qian*, he says lightly, for reading your fortune. Each *qian* is marked with a number in red, and placed into a bamboo holder. You shake the holder until one pops out and drops to the ground. The old man over there will interpret the fortune that corresponds with the number. I eye the thin reeds everywhere on the ground and the old man sitting in a corner, wearing dark sunglasses and a long white beard. Do I want my fortune told? Aunt Ung leaves us for a moment and comes backs with a handful of long yellow sticks of incense. Ang pulls out a lighter, lights all the ends and hands them out to us, three for each person, Dad looks faintly embarrassed; the sticks look very small in his hands. I look to Yun quickly, unsure of what we should do.

He gestures for us to follow him, and we line up behind others already kneeling.

"The idea is to be respectful. Thankful", Yun says. "You step up, plant the incense in the urn, and come back and pray for something."

Sylvain says he looks like an air hostess giving out emergency escape instructions, and Yun whacks him over the head with incense. Sylvain, with his arms over his head, backs into Chloe, whose incense goes flying. Hurriedly, Sylvain tries to redeem himself but her three scrawny sticks are quickly trampled by a group of passing children. After barely a moment, Sylain offers her his, holding out his hand to her, incense quivering. Chloe looks up at him and – as a few of us notice – blushes and takes it shyly. Olivia and Chloe are the first ones to plant their incense sticks, quickly stepping backward and then closing their eyes tightly, Olivia's lips moving almost despite herself. Out of the corner of my eye, I realise Sylvain is watching Chloe in a way I've never encountered before, as she kneels quietly, earnestly asking for things dear to her heart. What is she asking for? Yun catches my eye, smiling in an almost knowing way and tells me to go on. It seems I am always the last. Hesitating slightly, I move forward and stick my incense into the sandy base of the urn, the smoke stinging my eyes keenly. I step backward, taking care to keep facing forward and then clap my hands together, bowing my head. My mind is blank. I pretend to close my eyes, but from just beneath my eyelids, I watch as Olivia gets up, Yun taking her place. He goes through the motions swiftly, at ease, his face a mask of peace as he murmurs quickly and then joins Olivia. What am I thankful for?

Somewhere outside, the snow is still falling on the morning of our first Chinese New Year's day in a temple. I am thankful for this day.

***

It was still raining in the morning. I woke to the strains of *Georgia on My Mind* in my head. The day had dawned more quickly and starkly than I had ever thought possible and vaguely, skeleton-like, last night's words racked the hollow centre of my dreamless sleep. I clung to my bed-sheets and rolled back into the dip my body had made during the night and lay there for as long as I possibly could, counting my heartbeat against the slow tempo of *Georgia*. Somewhere at the back of my mind, I could smell sandalwood, the scent from the cupboards I hid in when Yun and I pretended to be ninjas, the light-footed, hooded assassins of Aunt Ung's many stories, the crack of a door opening, and a shaft of light catching me unawares. Perhaps. Perhaps there was still time. Minutes, maybe hours later, the door to my room creaked open slowly. Then, after a few moments.

"'Morning." It was Chloe.

I didn't answer, feigning sleep, my back to the door. She came and sat on the edge of my bed, my body shifting as the mattress accommodated her slight weight.

"'Morning", she repeated softly. "Still raining."

Then after another pause, she asked, "Did you sleep well?"

"I couldn't sleep", I finally answered, my voice muffled, turning to face her. In the half dark of my room, I could make out the edge of her jaw, and a resigned turn of the head.

"Neither could I."

"Did you dream?"

"I can't remember, I must have."

We were both quiet then, the interrogator and the interrogated. She reached out and brushed a strand of hair away from my face.

"Are you hungry?"

I shook my head against the pillow.

"I'll go make some breakfast anyway", Chloe offered. "I went out and bought some food just now. It's going to be a long day." She sat there a while longer, staring at that spot on the floor. Then, I wondered, as she left the room as quickly and quietly as she had entered, if she had been on the verge of saying more, because she had clearly come in knowing I would be awake. I had known Chloe almost longer than I knew myself, in fact her infant face in my mind's eye was probably more distinct than my own; to be mistaken identities was to be closer to each other than to one's own heart.

And yet. Words now hung in the air. Rickety and ruinous.

I sat up with a wooly struggle, staring at the closed door. With a sigh, I remembered I had yet to write the eulogy and, after checking the time, I saw I had only four hours to write it. Shrugging on an old sweater, I made my way through the chilly house to the kitchen where Chloe had already put on the coffee and was toasting some bread. An empty glass vase, its bottom round and bulbous, standing in the middle of the kitchen table. In her pink terry hoodie, Chloe looked more a part of the house than I did, a mother playing house in suburbia.

"I haven't written the eulogy yet", I confessed from the kitchen table, tucking my legs under me.

"I know," Chloe answered, opening the fridge and extracting three eggs I noticed. "But eat first. I haven't cooked for you in a while."

We both stepped eagerly into the refuge of domesticity, a no-man's land between territories, and potentially littered with mines. Soon the kitchen was filled with the smell of eggs frying and toast. Chloe was an excellent cook and it had been a while since she had cooked for me, it was true. In contribution, I put on the radio, flipping through channels till we reached some decent music, the tunes from *Sunday Kind of Love* swirling in the air.

Behind us, outside the kitchen windows, mist hovered, and raindrops fell from a pebble-grey sky. In the swing of winter, no sunlight seemed to penetrate the mid morning gloom. Reaching for the third egg, Chloe commented placidly on the lack of food in the house. Gamely, I admitted to a lacklustre performance in the kitchen department, a blatant waste of our brochure-perfect kitchen. Chloe, I said lightly, you should be married by now. Startled, her hand slipped and with a *damn*, the egg dropped and oozed through its cracked shell on the floor. Hastily, she scooped it up and tossed it into the trash can. She took a wet cloth and wiped at the floor angrily, a strand of streaked blonde hair falling out of the short pony-tail at the nape of her neck. A surprising vehemence. Another egg from the fridge, straight into the pan where it sizzled loudly. She nudged at the contents with a wooden spatula, the other hand on her hip.

I was seeing someone.

Blankly I looked at Chloe, uncomprehending. Abruptly.

"But I'm not anymore." She took a deep breath. "He fired me."

"What?" Maybe it was too early in the morning but I was failing to understand. And then it was too late.

"What I told you yesterday… About the column… I'm trying to explain to you..." She took another deep breath. "I worked for him. We dated. Then he fired me."

Her finish was brusque.

Then, the white settled. We had gone from eggs to men in less than a heartbeat. Automatically.

"Oh, Chubs." Did you love him?

Does it matter?

Of course it does.

Then Chloe said in a fifty-year-old's voice, Everyone loves. Love, it's everything and nothing and could be anything. Mostly, it's just a word for a time and a place and an inclination. Everyone loves. It's how it ends that matters, right? She held the spatula suspended over the pan, refusing to meet my eyes.

And so it goes.

"I just wanted to tell you before you heard it from someone else. That's why I don't work at the paper anymore." She turned her back on me, all squared shoulders. Is it ever possible to read a person's back, through a bathrobe and years of practiced armour? That familiar back, say, in these very lines of muscle and bone and tendon and skin, did this back say, I have it in me to weather this storm because I am strong, I need no pity shrouded in sympathy and I will emerge victorious though it may hurt. Or did that back say, don't touch me, don't even look at me or I may just fall apart, this egg-shell armour, piece by thousand piece and even if I am put back together, the pieces will be in the wrong place, so don't touch me.

When you can't read a back.

Then Olivia entered. If she sensed the awkward tension in the air, she chose not to show it.

"Morning", she said, standing by the counter, her hair still a little tousled from sleep.

Morning, I almost squeaked, over-compensating. Chloe said nothing, dishing the eggs.

Chloe wordlessly brought the eggs and toast to the table in two large plates. One, two, three perfectly rounded, sparingly oiled fried eggs. In the early light of day, all revelations big and small seemed less harmful. In the face of Chloe's brightly coloured eggs or Olivia's slender form, her face yet untouched by the ravages within. In the early light of day, I hoped for momentary peace. And so it could have been the seed of an olive branch or it could be Chloe mothering Olivia's child but neither made any obvious statements. I got up to pour out mugs of brew as Olivia took her seat at the table gingerly. She shivered slightly, cold through the material of the thin shift she had slept in and dutifully rubbed the sleep from her eyes like a cat might lick its injured paws. Chloe had produced a full pot of fresh coffee, from where, I had no idea. Fetching three mismatched mugs, I lined them up on the counter. Chloe took coffee with a pack of Equal and a dash of skimmed milk, I reminded myself, whereas Olivia liked hers black. I had always preferred tea, but since coffee had already been made and I had no idea when I had last purchased tea, I made myself some with a generous amount of milk. I brought the mugs over to the table on a small tray. Somewhere, Chloe had dug up place-mats and arranged the cornflower blue rectangles in a pattern of regularity. Jam was laid out in a small dish next to the butter, a spoon and a butter knife by their sides. In this playhouse of ours, I caught the scent of Chloe's carefully orchestrated lines of conduct. The more of a mess our real lives were, the tighter Chloe pursed her lips and straightened place-mats, organized CDs in alphabetical order, ironed handkerchiefs. In the midst of a hurricane, not one hair on Chloe's head would be out of place. Still, conversation was hard to fabricate. I poked listlessly at my egg, the perfectly cooked yolk running quickly down the side, like lava down a mountain side.

"Does anyone have any ideas for Yun's eulogy?" I finally asked, unable to put it off for any longer.

Olivia's eyes darted to me, obviously surprised, her coffee-mug half way to her mouth. I was compelled to answer.

"I couldn't…it was…" I inhaled on every word. *Difficult.*

She nodded, taking me at my word.

"Did you want to say anything about the story-telling?" Chloe reminded me of yesterday's session, dabbing at the corner of her mouth with a napkin.

"Yes, but what should I say about it?"

"Maybe you could retell one of his favourite stories", Olivia suggested, neatly picking up the thread.

"There were so many," I said, my brow furrowed.

Olivia, "The story about two lovers stranded on separate stars, only able to meet once a year when the Milky Way creates a path between the two stars, perhaps too pretty a story to be told on this occasion."

Chloe, "The story about the poet who wrote poems lamenting the injustice in the country, who was condemned to death, his body cut into a hundred pieces and thrown into the river."

Olivia, "I thought he couldn't bear it, so drowned himself and the sympathetic villagers threw rice balls into the water so the fish wouldn't eat his body."

In my mind's eye, we are young and there is a table full of lotus leaves Aunt Ung is stripping to wrap sticky rice with.

Chloe, straightening place-mats, frostily, "That's what the boats were there for, *to scare the fish away.*"

"Let's not tell that story then", I broke in quietly, and the two clammed up immediately, chastised.

They were like porcupines in cold weather, huddling in close to keep warm but piercing each other with every shuffle. Another one of Yun's favourites. Like a maligned cat, Chloe picked up the empty plates and took them to the sink, one of them catching the counter top with an angry clank. Clang. Clang Clang. Olivia took another sip of her coffee, both hands around the mug. I was so weary. I wasn't even sure if they needed each other for warmth. Perhaps I was in the middle with a thousand quills in my sides and I would slowly bleed to death from an instrument like Jesus' crown of thorns.

A Painted Moment

"There's the one about the shadow", Olivia said suddenly, "The little girl and her shadow." She sought my eye. As if. Innocently. I looked away.

***

Thud. The bottle hits the damp ground and rolls at first slowly, then quickly down the incline. I watch it roll. They have yet to realize I am there.

It is a milky dark and I can just see Yun in the slight moonlight, his face starkly white. He holds his body at an alert angle, dressed in black, the effect as if his head is floating on the wind. There is a scuffling sound and Sylvain lurches into view, pelvis first followed by his shoulders and finally his feet, a wild caricature of himself. Yun reaches out to grab his shoulders so he won't trip down the slope, his hands closing on the fabric of Sylvain's t-shirt, but Sylvain shakes him off roughly.

"I'm fine." His voice is tinged with disgust.

"We don't have to do this", Yun says firmly.

Sylvain does not appear to hear. He fumbles. In the dark, I can't see what he's fumbling with. Then, a wide spot of light materializes as Sylvain switches on a torch and then, rustling, an old sheet of paper and a small saucer. I see Yun is shaking his head. As Sylvain leans to place the paper on a poor soul's headstone, he loses his balance and Yun has to reach out and steady him again.

I notice they are standing at the top of one of the steeper inclines of the cemetery built on the hill. There are a set of graves up here, just by a large tree with wide, sweeping branches. It's the view and the breeze and the quiet so we gather there, on a clear day, the almost precipice drops away to reveal the town and people scurrying like little ants. Yun and Sylvain settle down and place a small saucer bottom up on a sheet of paper. I realize what they are doing and decide this is probably the most appropriate time to reveal myself and so I trudge louder and seek a pebble to kick.

Yun looks up.

"You're here." His face, illuminated from below, is particularly eerie.

Sylvain squints at me.

"Hi", I say, reaching the fringes of the torch-light.

Sylvain nods and turns his attention back to the piece of paper while Yun gestures me to sit down. I don't. I have never liked this game. Nor does Yun, if I recall; but Sylvain needs Yun to read the paper. The thin delicate piece of paper is covered in intricate Chinese characters organized into segments like a *fengshui bagua*; in the centre is a space for the upturned saucer. The writing spirals out in a mesmerizing pattern. Yun looks at Sylvain and down at the age-old paper, perhaps cursing Ang for the day he dug up the *die xian* from the recesses of one of Aunt Ung's old wooden trunks.

Sylvain places the tips of his fingers on the base of the saucer and closes his eyes, his eyeballs moving beneath his eyelids. I remain standing, my arms crossed, my sense of skepticism not entirely overcome by a cold, slow chill that runs the entire length of my spine and ruffles the fine down on the back of my neck.

The torch-light rolls a little and wind grazes the tips of the grass.

And then the saucer begins to move, slowly but surely, in gentle fits, the saucer leaves the centre of the paper and tracks a line to a set of characters. The saucer stops. Sylvain does not open his eyes but leans into Yun.

Yun looks at the paper, pain in his expression, and there is a damp silence.

"Syl?"

"Just read it!"

"No."

"Just... Read it!" Sylvain opens his eyes and even in the half dark, we see they are bloodshot.

"*Li Bie*", Yun says shortly. Departure.

Sylvain looks down at the paper and I hold my breath. He closes his eyes again, and there is nothing but the wind and the grass and the pain that singes. The saucer does not move again, we wait but there is no movement. Finally, Sylvain slumps and he gazes forward.

"Are you sure?"
Yun nods.
Now. Say it Now.
"Syl."
What?
"Her mum walked out on them yesterday," I say quietly, "I came to tell you that. May be now, well, I think. Just don't hate her."
Sylvain stares at me and I am proud of myself because I hold my ground. And then in one swift move he picks up the torch and kicks it, it soars and an arc of light cuts through the air before it hits the ground and rolls rapidly down the slope. We are left in the dark with our silence. *Li Bie*. Departure.

***

My sweating hands were leaving marks on the piece of paper I clutched so tightly. I felt distinctly ill. I wished I hadn't eaten those eggs. The three of us had cobbled together the story of the girl and the shadow, Olivia remembering the least, Chloe insistent. *My name is Rachel Glass. Yun and I have been friends for twenty years.* None of us had known what to say after the story, though Chloe contended I had to say something about how he would wish to be remembered. She had turned away when I said plainly that I had no idea how he wanted to be remembered. I stared hard at the paper, trying to focus on what I would have to say, but the words began to uncoil and separate, changing and spinning like turning prayer-wheels covered in Sanskrit. I looked up. Looked back down. Looked up again. Inappropriately, I could hear Olivia's voice from the next room, talking to Will, the cadence of her voice strained, lies already being spun.
"What are you doing?"
Chloe stood in the doorway in a sleek black suit. Her clothes were always tailored, a constant reminder of the baby fat she had shed since high school.
I looked at her mutely.
"You're not dressed yet." She checked her watch.
"Do you know the words to *Georgia on My Mind*?"

Chloe stared at me as if she could hardly believe what was on my clearly lost mind.

"Rache?"

"It's one of my favourite songs."

The back of her hand went to her mouth fleetingly, before she walked over to me and put the same hand on my shoulder.

"You need to get dressed."

Chloe shooed me into the shower, turning on the shower water for me, clucking at my purple toe-nail from my mishap yesterday morning. As I stepped into the shower, she kept up an unending commentary on the state of my room, my closet, my clothes. "Everything you have is the same, Rache!" And "Do you live in jeans these days? Honestly". When I emerged wrapped in a towel, Chloe had already laid out a set of clothes and was regarding them with pursed lips, her nervous chatter fading in my presence. Just because she was having other troubles did not mean she could not mobilize me into a forward momentum. She took another towel and vigorously dried my long hair, wringing out the ends. I put on the black shirt and pants she told me to as she tried to blow-dry my hair. Chloe said I would freeze, the whir of the hair-dryer drowning her out as she grappled unsuccessfully, brush in hand, with my slightly unkempt hair. Giving up, she caught the length of it back into a neater pony-tail. She stepped back to look at me appraisingly and grudgingly held out the arms of a trench-coat she had dug up from the recesses of my closet.

I don't think I can do this, I whispered.

For a moment, her eyes softened as they held mine. Then she shook her head, holding out the trench-coat again, the moment past.

"I wish you didn't have to," she told me, picking out strands of my fringe to frame my face, the gesture so absent but intimate, "But you have to. And you can do it."

She gave me as peppy a smile as she could muster and a pat before ushering me into the trench-coat and out of the door.

We found Olivia waiting for us on the porch, her hands concealed in a faux-fur muffler, large sunglasses concealing her eyes despite the rain. The three of us cut dark figures under darker umbrellas as we walked out to the main road to catch a cab, puffing cold clouds in the air. Olivia asked me if I was alright. I shook my head, feeling the way I felt before I got onto a plane or rollercoaster, the pit of my stomach clenching and unclenching like the pulsing centre of an oyster.

It was a short distance to the main cemetery half way up the hill, a distance I would have walked in better weather, but as it was, our cab took the opposite route, away from Wiseys, behind the hill. Silent for a while behind fogged-up windows, we passed streets of shuttered houses, colourful in the sun, wasted in the rain, an ancient bridge over the gorge where water swollen from the rain gushed against rocks, the bridge creaking with every revolution of the cab's tires. Olivia remarked on the ghost-like quality the day had assumed; everywhere it seemed, souls had fled leaving an imprint of being, like the umbrellas that stood tightly shut against the rain on cafe tables. The island's ancient trees, lining every one of the island's roads, hid us from prying eyes at every turn. These pines stood tall and taller, reaching up and away from our grief that poured like tar onto the ground. It was so very ashen, this day.

All too soon, our ride passed the first group of mourners on the road, their faces smudged through the windows even as Chloe wondered aloud who they were, all identical in funeral shrouds. Like one of the *Godfather* movies. As I got out of the cab, the grass in front of me was awash in funeral black, the number of characters in black seemingly multiplied by the dark umbrellas held above their heads. This was my first funeral. And so it was hard to know what happened next, where to go and what to do, so we followed.

Slowly, our heels sinking ever so slightly, we walked up the tree-lined incline as the rain came down around us, peppering the ground, until the little path turned into grass and mud and we pushed a little harder up the hill. I noticed Josh and Sylvain walking up in front, just as they noticed us, their silhouettes elongated in black suits, cigarettes hanging off their lips, while Glory in a long, narrow skirt, two steps for every one of theirs, hurried to keep up. Sylvain turned and waited for us, pulled his hand out of his pocket and offered his arm to Chloe. She hesitated for what seemed the longest of times and then took it, and together we kept walking. The crisp cold air, usually so refreshing, seemed to choke my lungs, leaving me gasping finite gulps, the way I feel when I dive into a pool during the winter, the moment contact steals your breath away. I sought to concentrate on that, in breathing in and out, on the feel of the ground beneath me, on the mouths of acid air that burned their way through my body and numbed my fingers.

Near the very top of the incline, two lines of chairs were arranged next to an incongruous signpost in the ground bearing a large number five. The chairs were covered with protective plastic jackets under which a man in a big hat and a black raincoat hastened to slip sheets of paper, an umbrella hanging from the right angle of his arm dragging in the mud. No one sat, but groups of three or four standing together (perhaps recognizable?), talking in low voices or else looking around uncomfortably, unwilling to let eyes meet or speak too loudly. The collective evasiveness seemed vaguely familiar, a jacket to be slipped on too easily or a fog that descended slightly. At Sylvain's request, Chloe and he moved off to one side, away from the crowd, talking in low voices. I noticed that the man in the big hat had stopped and was looking at me. It was another moment before I realized that he was going to come and talk to me and that I should know him.
"Rache."
"Yes, Oli?"
"You know you have to speak to that man now."
"Yes, Oli."
The man had arrived in front of me, his umbrella still sticking out strangely.
"Miss Glass? You remember me from the…the funeral home?"
"Yes. Of course. Yes I do."
"Is the family with the coffin?"
I looked around to see if that was the case but neither family nor coffin was anywhere to be seen. "I…"

"Yes, I believe so", Olivia cut in.

The man cleared his throat and I saw that he was sweating in this cold and that he had a handkerchief tucked into his sleeve.

"You will be speaking later?" the man continued, "Before the family speaks?"

I nodded. I tried to say something more and had yet to form the words when my throat contracted without warning and my stomach heaved. I just managed to stumble far enough away to throw up in a puddle, cold sweat bursting on my brow. Olivia's one hand patted me on the back, the other holding up an umbrella above my head. Someone passed me a tissue for me to wipe my mouth with, while I bent over, clutching at my chest for as long as possible. Out of the corner of my eye, I saw that Chloe and Sylvain had stopped their urgent conversation and Chloe hurried over. In the near distance, the man with the big hat fanned himself.

"You know you don't have to do this", Olivia said to me as I straightened up, mortified.

"Yes she does", Chloe said a little breathlessly, "The Ungs are counting on her."

"I'm sure they'll forgive her", Olivia answered reasonably.

"It's not about forgiving her! It's her responsibility! They need her to do it!" Chloe retorted. "Think of all that the family has done for her!"

"It's not about forgiving? It's all about that!"

"There are things in life that one is obligated to do!"

"Not that many things!"

"How can you say that?"

"Why not? There is more to life than obligation!"

"I'm sure that's what you would say. Do me a favour; Don't try to pass yourself off as the only one with feelings." This last, through pressed lips.

And then, "It's too late now!" said Olivia.

And it was. I saw people break their strides as they turned in deference to the hearse that had finally driven up. They both became silent, arguments becoming pointless as men in suits got out of the car and moved around to open the back doors.

Following the men, came first Uncle and then Aunt Ung, emerging warily but determinedly. I saw that Aunt Ung had on the hat my mum had sent from Spain, and for a moment I was able to set aside why she was wearing it and admire the effect. The hat was an array of short dark veil just covering her chin, dusted with gleaming dark feathers and curved around, molding to the shape of her stately head. Below the hat, she wore a cheongsam of the deepest colour underneath a heavy black cape. Perhaps it was not seeing her face clearly, or maybe it was the erect way she held herself, but Aunt Ung seemed a different person, closely bottled and regal. Pacing herself to match the pall-bearers, Yun's coffin held aloft to move before her, she followed at a slow pace. The coffin seemed slightly tilted to one side where they had two men instead of the three on the opposing side, and I realized with a sudden jolt that they had saved a space for Ang. His absence, up until this moment I had largely managed to forget. But seeing the uneven distribution made me suddenly indignant.

The procession made its way up and forward, slowed by the sodden ground, gradually approaching the chairs and the man in the hat and the raincoat, now standing somberly at the head of the arrangement in greeting. A straggle of female relatives welcomed Aunt Ung into their fold, and I was reminded briefly of the story of the seven swans, all huddled around Aunt Ung in her regality. I thought again of the man in the hat and when he had visited the Ungs two weeks ago at their house, from the funeral home, charged with running through procedure and presenting options. The Ungs had chosen the simplest option – without readings from the bible, without elaborate ceremony. The man had not seemed surprised at their muteness and I didn't remember his name.

"Is that the hat your mum sent?" Chloe murmured as we were swept along.

I nodded.

"It's beautiful."

It seemed everything had been washed black and white by the rain. I saw Sylvain, Josh and Glory take seats in the second row, cigarettes abandoned, hands now clasped in front of them. The three of us moved to the front row and took seats to one side. Over the tops of other guests' heads, I could see Aunt Ungs' feathers. The coffin was brought to rest directly above a freshly dug hole, the pall-bearers stepping away and taking their places in the congregation, Uncle Ung last of all, lingering by the coffin, his body slightly stooped. Aunt Ung called to him softly and he moved in broken jerks towards her; a background keening, an unbroken chain of tears and low moans started then, subdued by the rain.

What do you do when someone leaves you? Where does the love go when there is nothing in front of you but empty air and colder dreams?

The man (what was his name?) stood forward at the head of Yun's coffin and cleared his throat, addressing us as dear friends, his eyes moving rapidly so he could look at everyone and no one at the same time. He was wrong, the harsh way he pronounced their surname with a nasal "g" sound at the end; a priest would have been worse, but he was all wrong.

Chloe squeezed my hand, her hands cold as ice, bringing me back. I couldn't tell from beneath Aunt Ung's hat if she was crying. Maybe she wasn't.

"Rache, I think you're up soon", Olivia whispered in my ear. On cue, the man came towards me, proffering his umbrella. My shoes squelched in the grass as I stepped forward and turned to face the group, tied to the man for the shelter his umbrella offered. I squinted at the faces in front of me, unconsciously scanning them for any chance of comfort. I could see Glory's comforting arm, with some difficulty, around Josh's large burly frame as he wiped at his tears with a checkered handkerchief. Aunt Ung's sisters, all three of them in the front row, who in their black attire reminded me of old crones. James Aimes had slipped in next to Sylvain, his hair slicked back out of what must have been respect. Sylvain, still not clean shaven, looked ready for work in a black suit and black tie.

My name is Rachel Glass. Yun and I have been friends for twenty years.

A Painted Moment

I heard the slight chink of metal against metal and saw James Aimes surreptitiously pass Sylvain a flask from which he quickly took a short but deep swig. James Aimes coughed, taking the flask back and replacing it in his inside jacket pocket. Chloe, perhaps smelling something, turned her head to look at Sylvain reprovingly, Sylvain straightening the cuffs of his shirt, the silver of his cuff-links gleaming. I fingered the piece of paper in my pocket and finally took it out. Joseph, a man Yun worked with at the local hospice, was looking faintly embarrassed in the fourth row, his hair swept to one side in an ill-fitting style.

My name is Rachel Glass.

"Anytime you're ready", the man said to me softly.

Uncle Ung had his arms tightly folded, his eyes burning holes into the coffin, did anyone notice he swayed slightly on his feet? Olivia's hands were still tucked inside the muffler, her wheat blonde hair lifting slightly with the wind, her eyes inscrutable, an ocean of space between Chloe and her. Amherst was here, a black bowler hat and a Duke Ellington black record clutched to his chest, eyes downcast. Josh crying into a checkered handkerchief, Glory playing the role of comforter. Aunt Ung's three sisters as crones. James Aimes and his hip flask filled, his hair slicked back. Sylvain taking a quick swig, Chloe always mindful, disapproving. Joseph with his bad hair style.

"Miss Glass?"

Uncle Ung swaying to his own beat. Olivia hidden behind large sunglasses. Amherst and Duke Ellington. I unfolded the piece of paper and looked down at it, tiny black ants forming hieroglyphs unread in my hands. I looked back up at Aunt Ung. She could have been trying to say something to me, her body still, her head turned towards me, obscured behind a façade of black and feathers. Josh and Glory, three crones, James and his flask, Chloe disapproving of Sylvain, Joseph, Uncle Ung's pain, Olivia's sunglasses, Amherst and Duke Ellington.

Cold water rose up all around me. Spanish lace.

Yun and I have been friends for twenty years.

***

A Painted Moment

Sixteen.

I crane my neck and step on tip-toe. I count the number of people in front of me again. Sixteen. My heart is pounding in my chest and I furiously start praying that our school will catch on fire so we can all leave. Maybe the nurse will spontaneously combust, I've seen it happen in cartoons I watch at weekends. I crane my neck again. Sixteen still.

My eyes fall on a head of wiry black hair. Yun, almost at the front of the line, doesn't seem scared at all, looking around at everything curiously, wide-eyed. We met yesterday morning at the bus-stop, with his brother (I can't pronounce his name), and his mum who wore a funny dress with a high collar around her neck, just under her chin, nothing like what Mum has, it's blue with black flowers.

It is sunny and early and I am still slightly dopey, my fingers still sticky from strawberry jam on toast. The two boys arrive in a cloud of dust and short breath, a kind voice calling ahead in a language that makes my dad turn his head curiously, my blue and green school-bag tiny and light in his hands.

"Good morning. You must be our new neighbour." Dad is friendly and stretches out his free hand.

The lady smiles politely.

"Ung." Her voice is gentle and light. She points at the little boys who look at us with big round eyes, scuffling. "My sons. Ung Ang and Ung Yun."

Dad smiles back cheerfully.

"Jonathan Glass," He grabs me by the scruff of my neck, "This is Rachel, my daughter."

The pretty lady smiles at me. I shrink behind Dad's leg.

"Your family should come over for dinner some time. We would like to welcome you to the neighbourhood," Dad says jovially. "Bring your sons! We make a very good lasagna." He doesn't yet know that it will be Aunt Ung who hosts mouthwatering dinners in the years to come.

"Thank you," the lady answers, still smiling. "Very kind."

Their conversation is cut short by the arrival of our school bus, and we are herded on like stray calves into a barn, Aunt Ung hugging each son, dad patting me on the head and handing me my school-bag.

"Yun. Ung Yun."

I turn my head to see that Yun is sitting across the aisle, swinging his legs, a big smile on his face.

"Yung Un." I try to mimic him but fail.

"Yu-uuu-un."

"Yu-uuu-un." My tongue pushes against my bottom teeth.

He nods, then looks at me expectantly. I realise he is waiting for me to reciprocate.

"Rachel", I say carelessly. "Rachel."

"Rachel." He is perfect on his first attempt. I turn away, ashamed, pushing away his friendly overture. At six years of age, I am chilly and my pride is wounded.

Standing in the queue now, I realize that Yun has turned and is looking at me closely. I blink. He tries smiling, but his smile wanes when he realises how scared I am. His face takes on a thoughtful expression before our Mrs Wilkins, a mountain of flesh and orange stockings, whisks him away to be tended to by the nurse. I strain my ears for the sound of screaming or sobs, but there is none and Yun soon reappears with a large band-aid on his arm, a red lollipop in his hand and a white note clutched between his fingers.

Fourteen.

Gulp.

As Yun passes me, he stealthily doubles back and gets in line behind me, me who cowers at the back of the line.

"Lollipop?" He asks quietly as he hands it to me. I take it blankly. He then hands me the note he is carrying and steps in front of me. For a moment, I stare at his back, uncomprehending. I look down at the note on which is written no name, simply our class (Mrs Wilkins), our age, the horrible word measles and then the words CLEARED stamped in red at the bottom. I look back up at Yun, who seems oblivious to my presence, one shoe scratching the back of the other leg.

The sheer genius of his plan reveals itself in all its blinding glory. I feel like kissing the ground.

A Painted Moment

So, as naturally as possible, I wheel around, put as much distance as I can between myself and the nurse's station, and walk back towards our classroom, falling in step with prissy Clarissa Gammon, brandishing the big red lollipop with happy relief. Deception comes easily to me at this young age too, not just pride. Before I turn the corner, I steal a glance back and see that Yun has rolled up his other sleeve and is almost at the front of the line, blissfully at ease.

"How was your injection, Rache?" Dad has his hand on my head as I'm separating the layers of my lasagne so I can pick out the pepper-corns.

I swallow and then stuff a big bite into my mouth so I don't have to talk.

Dad ruffles my hair, Brave Girl!!!

I smile with my mouth full. Do I feel guilty? Not really.

The next morning at the bus-stop, it's still sunny. Dad walks me to the bus-stop as usual and we see that Ang is waiting with his mum but there is no sign of Yun. Fever, his mum says lightly, from the needle, the nurse says it happens sometimes. My dad nods knowingly and pats me on the head, like he is thankful my body hasn't reacted to the injection. I'm in shock. Fever?

Now I feel bad.

All the way to school, I am wracked with guilt, I imagine Yun on his deathbed, a towel on his forehead, sweat on his brow. I am restless that day at school, twisting the end of my sweater, wondering if I will be sent away for what I've done – unknowingly – but I've still done it. By the end of Mrs Wilkin's maths class, I have failed our fractions quiz and I am sure that Yun is uttering his last words, his mum holding his hand. I have to confess, I decide tearfully, I have to say sorry before it's too late. The bus-ride home is agonizingly long, I keep jumping to my feet to see if we're there. I fly off the school bus and run down the road to the Ungs. I stop on the porch, swallowing, cowed by the imposing door. Before I can knock, the door swings open slowly and Yun's mum is standing just inside the doorway.

"Rachel." Her voice is like silver bells and she smiles as she bends close to my face.

"I'm sorry!" I burst into tears. "I didn't mean to kill him!"

She is not bewildered, not as she ushers me into the house and gives me pretty lavender slippers to wear (they are too big for me), not as she leads me quietly up the stairs, not as she opens the door to Yun's bedroom to reveal him propped up in bed. She knows, I think as she leaves us, she knows.

"Hi!" Yun is surprised but pleased to see me, putting aside his chess board. A blanket is tucked around him and two or three pillows surround him.

I stand by the door, pigeon-toed, face wet with tears. He beckons for me to sit on the bed but I am so sorry I can't bring myself to look at him.

"Rachel?"

"I'm so sorry, I was just scared, I'm really sorry," I say in the smallest voice that I have.

"Hurt only a little", Yun says brightly.

"How are you now? Do you still have a fever?" I'm quiet.

"Better", he says easily.

Slightly comforted, I sniffle. I sneak a look at him, he's smiling at me. They really are an awfully smiley family.

"Still afraid?"

I shake my head, no, the dangers of gleaming needles far behind me now.

"Do you know how to play Chinese chess?"

"Chinese chess?"

"Chinese chess", Yun nods, "Come. Let me teach you."

I hesitate for one split second, then I cross the room to sit on the end of his bed. Yun puts the board across his knees between us, picking up the wooden pieces and rearranging them. The door creaks and Aunt Ung comes in with a jug of fruit tea and glasses on a tray, she puts her hand on my shoulder and she smiles at me again.

Years later, I sit in my doctor's waiting room, flipping through a magazine, waiting for a check-up. Out of nowhere, between an ad for nicorette and an article on hepatitis, the image of Yun giving me his lollipop comes back to me, his funny face while he's tucked in bed. My hero already, and only six.

Anyway, after that, Yun is my best friend. How can you not be best friends with someone who takes a needle for you?

I dreamed in red

Her voice came to me like waves lapping gently at the shore. There were tiny white pebbles in the soil underfoot that was quickly turning into mud. It was Aunt Ung's voice. I realised that I was lying down across two chairs, my face sticking to the plastic. Aunt Ung was standing next to the man with the umbrella, her face still obscured, a rose in her hand. I watched her walk over to the coffin, leave the rose on the lid and lay her hand on it. Behind me, someone broke out into a loud sob that was quickly stifled. For a minute, there was nothing but the rain and my breathing and my face stuck to the chair, as Aunt Ung, joined by Uncle Ung, turned and slowly walked away from their son. Around me, people began to break from the group. Some walked to the coffin, others left quickly, for fear of too many tears perhaps, for their cars. Just people streaming past.

At a distance, there was a flurried discussion, Chloe insisting that she would take care of me and for Aunt Ung to go back to the house with the other guests. Aunt Ung seemed to argue for a moment before giving in. I closed my eyes and drifted, delaying the actual moment when I would have to sit up and respond and interact.

"Rache?" Chloe's voice was at my ear.

I heard Glory tell Josh to take the boys to Uncle Ung's first.

The funeral was over.

"How are you feeling?"

Gingerly, I pushed myself back into a sitting position and put a hand to my head. Beaten cotton. Chloe stood next to me, sheltering me from the rain with an umbrella.

"What did I do?" I finally asked, in a voice that did not seem to be my own.

Chloe looked away, strained, and Glory shifted from foot to foot. No one wanted to look at me, it seemed.

"Nothing." Olivia's face came into focus, her voice firm, "Nothing. You were very dignified in your silence. It's a good thing the guy caught you."

It was meant to be a comforting thought. The sound of the rain grew, and in my head, it was like tribal drums, feet flapping on mud. I had the impression of whirling dervishes dressed in black as the last of the people filed past me. The mortification would probably set in later.

"Did anyone take my place?"

"Yes. I did", Olivia responded, sitting down next to me. I was mildly surprised.

"Did you read from my paper?"

She shook her head.

"I read some Bukowski."

"Bukowski?"

"I had it in my bag." Olivia paused. "I thought it more appropriate than what we'd worked on in the morning. What we worked on in the morning was more for you."

It was. The question of why Olivia was reading Bukowski would pop up later.

Beneath the incessant rain, I noticed another sound, the grinding of the gears. "I'm sorry", I heard myself say.

"You have nothing to be sorry about."

"I'm still sorry."

The three of them stood there, holding umbrellas, almost comic, unsure of what to say, as was I, I who had nothing to offer besides my apologies. The sound of the gears stopped abruptly. Moments later, ping, the unmistakable sound of soil hitting the coffin.

I flinched as if I'd been punched. They were burying Yun.

When we were eleven, Yun's labrador Oliver died, so he and Ang had written a poem, a poem that Yun read aloud at its funeral. Uncle Ung had dug a deep hole in their garden, and he stood there, leaning on the shovel, sweat glistening on his brow, as Aunt Ung laid the dog's body into the hole. Ang had his arm tightly clamped around Yun, who cried the whole time they buried Oliver, his tears making wet splotches on the white paper of the poem. I was there too. But I had sat on the back porch, watching from afar, for some unknown reason frightened, not daring to look into the hole, but still wanting to be there to provide some sort of support, no matter how removed. Whatever it might be. Ping. They were burying Yun.

My eleven-year-old self got up from the back porch steps and wished I would do something.

Rache...
Rachel, what are you doing?
To do something outside of your own control is when your heart and your head and your arms and legs all seem to look away as one or none of the above decides to spring to life and take control. So before my head or my heart can make sense of it, my feet are carrying me forward. Two men in dark raincoats stand by the open pit, one short fat man with a shovel, the other reedy with a prominent Poirot moustache, looking on as the other works, a clip-board under his arm. The man holding the shovel looks up in surprise, an exclamation dying on his lips as I lunge for the fat man's shovel.
"What the hell...? Miss, what d'you think you're doing? Get...".
The fat man stumbles backwards, taking me and the shovel with him.
We flail, my grip on the shovel slipping. I feel hands on my arms.
"You can't." I am desperate. "You can't...can't throw dirt on him."
"What d'you mean I can't? It's my job, Miss!" He splutters, struggling to keep his footing, the heels of his shoes digging into the ground.
"Rachel!" Arms come around my waist.
"Stop!" For all the world, my scream seems to cut through the rain, surely somewhere, someone will be stopped by my piercing voice. "Stop it! Stop shoveling!"
The fat man's face has gone quite red as he holds steadfastly, righteously, to his shovel, the moustache man co-worker looking back and forth between us like a spectator at a tennis game,

obviously floored. I kick wildly as my friends drag me back from the poor man, mud springing up on his pants and raincoat, the wildest I ever remember being, the closest to crazy I have ever come. The rain is on my face.

"Rache, please."

"Let go of me!" My heart resists as they kept pulling me away, farther and farther from Yun. "They can't do that! Let got of me!"

"Rachel, honey, shhhh. It'll be ok, come away now."

The fat man shakes his head, picks up his speed, just in case the crazy girl returns, at least he can say he did his job. The moustache man watches my friends drag me away, his big eyes sad and almost wistful, his moustache drooping. Perhaps I will stand a chance with him. Olivia and Chloe push me back against a large tree, trying to hold me to the trunk. We are all soaked, umbrellas upturned and forgotten behind us, rolling in circles on the ground.

"You have to stop them! How can you let them do that?" I am yelling at them now. With sudden clarity, I realize how good it feels to holler so that fresh air seems to charge its way down my vocal chords. I wave my arms around and think, how great, how great it feels just to wave my arms and not care.

"It's their job and it's raining. They have to do it quickly", Chloe says reasonably.

"I have to go see him, I didn't look at the coffin. I haven't even looked at the pit yet, let me go, let me go!"

"Rache, stay. It will be alright."

I round on her.

"I won't stay! How can you say it will be alright when it's obviously the least right thing to ever happen? How can you possibly say that?!"

It is a dramatic moment, a scene from a soap opera played right out on the lawns of the cemetery, with two undertakers as witnesses, me the central character, me who has never been the centre of anything in my life, me who for the first time suddenly appreciates how good it feels just to yell.

I waved at my eleven year old self. She sat back down and watched Yun cry on Ang's arm.
Rache?
Chloe shook me by the shoulder. I turned to her slowly. She looked at me, worry knitted between her brows.
Let's go, shall we? It's getting cold and the rain will get worse. Come on, get up, let's go.
Everything was in red, I said.
Ping goes the shovel in the background.

***

You're supposed to grow old with the same people you were born with because you need someone to remind you what you are and who you're made of.

And if I said, she didn't mean to break his heart but did because she had to until she thought she was in love with someone else and then realized that he was in turn in love with someone who thought she was in love with him too until she wasn't sure if she was and realised she might have to break his heart. Would that make anything clearer? Would that remind her that she was made of him and he was made of her?

We were sitting in the Ung's kitchen at a long, dark-wood table that had just been cleared of food; I wondered when Aunt Ung had had the time to cook that much, plates of cold noodles and spring onions, stews of pork ribs in plum sauce, cucumbers dressed in garlic, and rows of soy chicken-thighs. It was a moveable feast to feed the starving, not the sad. Relatives dressed in black had descended like locusts upon the table, carrying it all away to feed those who had come to mourn some more. In the middle of the ceiling hung a large, round lamp woven from hundreds of thin red threads, a dexterous web, casting a low light across our fingers and arms. The setting had seen many a late night session. Many of the stories Yun told later were first told here by Aunt and Uncle Ung, their faces glowing red from the light. Large glass sliding-doors at the one end of the kitchen afforded views of the forest behind the house. The branches of the trees were suffering from the beating of the rain, jumping up and down like puppets on strings. Beyond the forest, there was nothing but a sea of mist and darkness. A low murmuring was coming from just outside the kitchen door. Despite my silence, my throat hurt in a way that I had never experienced before.

"Do you want anything to drink?" Olivia asked me, coming round to sit opposite me, slipping in between the table and the bench.

"Anything alcoholic would be nice", I answered wryly.

Glory offered to get it and we gratefully watched her push through the swinging door. I noticed Olivia already had a tumbler of whisky in front of her.

"I'm sorry. I feel like I blacked out."

"Virtually. Like I said, it's a good thing the guy caught you", Olivia responded, drinking from the glass. Ice-cubes clinked together; light bounced off her Turkish rings.

I didn't say anything. Olivia reached across the table and held my hand, demanding attention and focus.

"Hey."

I looked at her. I said I was sorry again.

"It's not a big deal", she told me firmly. "Really, on the larger scale of things."

She stopped mid-sentence as Chloe walked in, a towel and hot-water-bottle in one hand, a glass of wine in the other. Nonchalantly, Chloe came to me, draping a towel over one of my shoulders, announcing her intention to fill a hot water bottle. I looked around at our little group and realized that we had all stayed out in the cold longer than we ought. Thanks to my little black out, we were all slightly damp. She filled a cast-iron kettle with water and put it on the stove, looking around for a match to light the burner with.

"Do you want a lighter?" Olivia asked.

Chloe ignored her, finally locating a large box containing long, thin matches. I realized that Olivia's opposition to Chloe's view at the cemetery had again broken whatever tenuous bridge had been rebuilding between them. Olivia looked on calmly at Chloe's back, then took another sip from her glass. I thought she was going to ignore Chloe's behaviour, but then she took out a cigarette and lit it. She could have, as she had been doing for years. The acrid smell of smoke drifted over to Chloe, who stiffened.

"Do you want a lighter? You could have just said you don't", Olivia said, her voice light and heavy at the same time. "Do you want to talk? You can say no, too."

Chloe, hands on the counter, her fingers bending as she leant her weight on them, said nothing.

"Do you? Do you want to talk?"

I held my breath as I watched Chloe's back once again.

"Chubs?"

Chloe turned at that.

"Don't call me that – you of all people, do not call me that."

"I apologise." Olivia drew on her cigarette.

"You don't know what you're apologizing for."

"I can apologise for a lot of things."

"It takes a very special kind of arrogance to apologise for nothing and expect the other person to accept it."

Olivia had to pause and in spite of it all I had to give Chloe a point.

"I apologise for that too, then", Olivia countered.

Chloe seemed to move as if to turn away again but something kept her facing us. It could have been a window of opportunity or it could have been weariness in Chloe, a tiredness of the shoulders that bore the brunt of this burden. I held my breath. Somewhere, the wheels were turning slowly.

Quietly, Olivia said, "It doesn't have to be this way." She went on, "I'm sure we can work this out, if only we could talk about it. That's where we broke down, I'm sure."

"Are you? That's not where I think we broke down."

Olivia stared at Chloe, her cigarette burning away, and Chloe stared back at her, arms folded now and her jaw so set I fancied I could hear her creak. I tried to make myself as small as possible or shut my ears, I thought about leaving but couldn't tell which was worse.

"You don't get to win everything", Chloe said. "You don't get to win everything. *You don't get to win everything.*"

"Was I not paying attention? When did I win everything?"

They stared at each other again. Unspoken, in the air, hung a scroll of paper with a bright congratulatory ribbon round it. And then the shadow of a man approaching.

It took a few moments for Olivia to understand. And then.

"This isn't what I call winning", Olivia said, bitterness creeping into her last words.

Olivia, I murmured silently, don't say that, you can't mean it.

Chloe's eyes narrowed as she straightened herself to her full height. She tossed her hair and her nostrils flared before she said, with the fineness of threading a needle. You don't deserve that child.

Mum used to say that friends from childhood are friends for life, a thousand songs, a million books have been written about this. I used to think that too, but as I watched my two dear friends now, I realized how generous that assumption is and that it's more like the roll of a dice. If you're lucky, you come up with sixes every time, but you never know what losing combination you might possibly end up with.

As soon as the words were out of her mouth, I wondered if deep down, a younger, earlier, unscathed Chloe regretted saying it, as I watched Olivia stop, her long almond eyes registering Chloe's each and every word with the pain of a flame being snuffed out.

The kettle whistled, so she took it off the stove to complete her task of filling the hot-water-bottle. Steadily, she poured the water in and then screwed the cap back on. She handed it to me and for a long while, kept her hand on the bottom of the bottle, as the silence ticked through, thick and searing.

"Chubs", I whispered.

She let go and walked out of the kitchen. And so we were two.

I sometimes imagine, in silences, that I will say something brilliant and insightful, the sentences just form themselves and fly out of my mouth with ease. But something always stoppers this imagined capability and even though I wished more than anything I could say something to comfort Olivia, she had to be the one to speak first.

"I don't deserve this child?" It didn't feel as if her question was directed at me.

"That's not what she meant", I answered.

"Didn't she."

"No."

"It's possible."

I shook my head, pressing my lips together. "I'm going to get a drink."

"Let me come with you."

Earlier, we had arrived around the back of the house, unwilling to pass through what we knew would be a crowd gathered in the main part of the house. So our exit through the living-room was almost a shock, the elegant room filled with a throng of mourners, the size of the house suddenly reduced by the number of people dressed in black, sitting, standing, holding platefuls of food, gossiping, "so young" and "both sons", all gently swaying on a tidal wave of mourning that ebbed and swelled; the colour of their clothes seemed to absorb the colour of the art-work and the furniture around us. It was like switching the light out.

"I never thought the Ungs knew this many people", Olivia muttered, her glass held high above her head as she moved between groups of guests.

"It's the Chinese community", I answered, close behind her, feeling so out of place.

"Where's that bar?" Olivia scanned the living-room. "There."

We found Josh and James Aimes standing off to one side of a long table that served as a bar, drinks in hand, ties hanging low, looking as sorely out of place as we felt.

"My, aren't we a sight for sore eyes!" Olivia said, reaching for a bottle.

"Good thing you two are here," James Aimes was beyond the reach of any reproach. "We're getting pretty damn bored."

Josh grunted in such a way that I had to turn away from him.

As I did, my attention was caught by something. Something seemed off kilter. What was different? What was different about the...? There was the long wooden table, covered with a cloth, on top of which stood bottles of whisky, sake, wine, a bucket of ice, enough alcohol to floor a population of giants. The bar had been set up slightly in front and to the left of the bowl-shelf. Beyond and next to it, the Ungs' long wooden settees and brightly coloured pillows were unchanged, the white shell mobile still turned and tinkled lightly above our heads.

"We saw Chloe walk out", James said.

"Sylvain went after her?"

"Yes."

"But."

There was a shrug.

"Twenty-four hours of whisky could dismember anyone."

Olivia's eyes were trained on the boys, her thoughts hard to read. Was it that? The bowl-shelf? I moved in a little closer, then stood back to have a clear view of the entire shelf. Their brief exchange dissolved into the background. I counted.

"Rache? Are you ok?"

I didn't answer. Some of the bowls were missing. The fat round one with the green glaze. The small round one in black that fitted in the palm of my hand. I shouldn't even have needed to count, I realized. There were obviously half as many as there normally were.

"Rache?"

"The bowls", I muttered. "Some of the bowls are gone."

Olivia looked at me, then at the bowl-shelf, a blank expression on her face. It must have occurred to her at the moment that the grief might finally have been too much. I was grasping at straws now, irrelevant straws. She asked, slowly and distinctly, what I meant, the bowls were still there. Count them, I answered, count them. Some of the bowls are missing, someone must have taken them. The boys exchanged a look that infuriated me.

Listen, Aunt Ung said, as we listened in to that perfect silence, that is the most beautiful sound you will ever hear.

A Painted Moment

Shaking the cobwebs of memory from my head, I tried to explain myself.

"Listen! I'm not talking nonsense...", I was saying, when I was interrupted by a sharp nudge in the back.

"Excuse me." It was Mrs Wen, from the antiques store by the bay. I stepped out of her way, determined to make my point, when I saw her pick up a vase from a side-table next to me, look underneath it and then proceed to scribble something down on a piece of paper. The four of us looked on, not quite making head or tail of what old Mrs Wen was doing, the bowls forgotten. She tilted the vase up to the light, looking down her nose through the small lenses of the glasses perched on the tip of her nose. She narrowed her eyes as she turned the vase slowly, muttering to herself, until she realized we all four of us were watching her. She smelt, as did her shop, of mothballs.

"Yes? Is something the matter, children?" Mrs Wen asked, pushing her glasses up on top of her head and surveying us. All of a sudden we were all scruffily twelve, shuffling our feet, unsure of what to say. James Aimes looked up at the ceiling and almost whistled. She looked us up and down, and sniffed.

"Are you taking this?" Mrs Wen finally asked us waspishly.

"Taking the vase, you mean?" Olivia responded.

"Yes. The vase."

"Why would we be taking the vase?" I asked in confusion.

"Not taking it? Then stop wasting my time, you children," Mrs Wen said dismissively, bringing her glasses down again to study the vase once more. She bent over creakily to look at the side-table the vase was standing on, rapping on its wooden legs with bony knuckles, seemingly and puzzlingly testing their strength. I had never liked going into her store, something about her whippet thinness always scared me, but tonight I was bolder.

"I'm sorry, Mrs Wen, but why are you taking the vase?" I persisted.

"I'm not taking it, girl, I'm buying it. Buying the vase", Mrs Wen corrected me, making another note on her piece of paper. Presently, she paused, pushed her glasses up on top of her head again and straightened up to look at me.

"The Ungs are leaving", she said crisply. "You youngsters are aware of that, yes?"

After surveying our stunned faces, she shook her head.

"Well, now you know, and not a moment too soon. They're selling everything, that's why there's so many people here, yes?" Mrs Wen pursed her lips and turned away, moving on, her job done.

I watched her back for a moment, unable to process what she had said, the blood in my head pounding. I felt gazes on me and I turned to look back at my friends, all with pity and fear in their eyes, their fear not for themselves, I knew, but for me. What did I see in their eyes, surely not me that I saw in their eyes?

It is.

It's a beautiful sound.

The music that had formed the ground beneath me ceased to be and I fell through.

Abruptly, I wheeled away and blindly walked into the Paper Room, the very room where Aunt Ung had served me that simple meal just yesterday. I slid the door shut behind me, savouring the muffled silence the thin separation created. I walked over to the window, looking out, put my forehead against the cold, smooth surface, wondering what this meant, wondering what was happening to us in the Mr Hyde forms that our Dr Jekylls had now become. We were monsters. Without Yun, it seemed, the whole world had become monstrous. We had monsters amongst us and not the kind you found under the bed.

Hey.

It was Olivia,

I could see her reflection in the glass. I didn't say anything, kept my back to her.

"You should talk to them."

"What is there to say?"

"Plenty."

"I don't understand." I must have sounded like a stubborn child.

"Don't you?"

"It can't be true."

"It might be true", Olivia said carefully. We danced, choreographed, through sporadic bursts of talk as we came to know it might be true.

We knew it was. Out of the corner of my eye, I saw a box just next to my feet. Looking down, I realized that there were several boxes lined up on the floor next to some shelves at the end of the room, boxes that hadn't been in the room yesterday. Through the top of the box where the flaps didn't meet, I saw some black and white photos. Bending down, I pushed back the flaps of the box to get a better look.

"Oli. Look." I held out the top one to her.

It was a black and white photo of Yun and I at Wiseys. It must have been summer, what looked like more than ten years ago, he was helping me sort out a new order of books, the large doors to the garden were open, the curtains were lifting with the breeze and I could almost smell the fresh scent of cut grass. We were both sweating, laughing. Young.

As I passed her the photo, I turned to the other photos in what I realized was a small stack, mostly black and white, preserved inside a small, black box within the larger box. The next photo was of Aunt Ung and Yun asleep on deck chairs in the back yard during the fall, the black and white quality of the photo belying the beauty of a fiery red and gold evening and the mixed threads in the blankets that covered them.

Olivia wondered aloud if they were all Uncle Ung's photos, citing his love for black and white film.

I wasn't altogether sure. The next photo must have been taken during Chinese New Year. Uncle Ung had tied a long string of firecrackers to the ceiling of the porch and Aunt Ung was leaning forward to light the end of it, one hand over her ear, her body leaning to favour the hem of her patterned dress. I could just make out what looked like my back disappearing back into the house, running away from the loud bangs surely.

"That looks like you," Olivia told me, pointing over my shoulder. "Were we there?"

I nodded, scrutinizing the photo more closely.

"I'd almost forgotten how much bigger Ang was than Yun," Olivia murmured.

***

The sharp sound of something breaking makes me sit up like a jack in the box.

"What was that?" I ask, reaching out to shake Yun gently.

He has slid down in his chair and a book is resting open on his upturned face. Turning his head a fraction, the book drops, hitting the ground with a dull thud.

"Urumph," he grunts.

"Yun. I heard a sound like something breaking."

Yun doesn't say anything, still half asleep, perhaps he is dreaming.

Clang.

This time, it is his turn to sit up. I kick over a tall glass of tea in our haste to get into the house through the sliding doors.

"Stop that!" It is Aunt Ung's voice, trembling, barely a whisper. She stands between her husband and her eldest son, hands wringing at her dress.

I will never forget Uncle Ung's face, red with anger, a vein on his forehead popping up. Pieces of broken ceramic lie at his feet and he is bleeding just a little from his arm. In his hand, he clutches a letter.

"Ungrateful! "Uncle Ung spat. "You break your mother's heart."

On the receiving end is Ang, dry-eyed, jaw set, sitting on the edge of one of the chairs.

"I don't see her saying anything", he retorts quietly. "There's nothing wrong with what I want to do."

"After everything we've done for you, this is how you repay us?"

"It's what *you* wanted to do."

Every parent, with one hand over his heart, has to lie to his children at least once in his life. Uncle Ung is no exception.

"You and I are different."

"Not that different."

The silence presses down around us like the weight of water.

"Ang!" Yun starts towards his brother.

"Leave him!" Uncle Ung snarls. Yun casts a sharp look at his father.

"Ba, what – "

"That's right, just leave me alone", Ang cut in. Turning, he leaves the room. Moments later, we hear the front door close gently but firmly. Then the sound of a motor-cycle engine.

Aunt Ung's anxious words break over Uncle Ung like a wave cresting. Ignoring her, he too leaves to retire to his room. His heavy footsteps pace erratically the floor above our heads.

"That was at New Year", I finally pronounced. "Just before Ang left."

"Ang gave me his guitar pic." Yun turns the small triangle over and over in his hand.

"You don't play the guitar!" I laugh.

"I don't think that's why he gave it to me", Yun says slowly and I see an idea come to him like ice freezing in his eyes. "What time is it?" He clutches my arm.

"Quarter past ten."

"When's the next ferry?"

He doesn't wait for my answer. Yun turns and breaks into a run.

"I liked Ang," Olivia told me.

"A lot of people did," I answered softly.

"It seemed like such a long time ago and yet...not." She brought the photo close to her face. "Did they ever find out where Ang had gone?"

I shook my head, keeping quiet, not sure if I should speak lest I betray Yun even now. I looked at the photos in my lap and then back at the other boxes. I cast around the room, sizing up the other boxes, wondering if I should look at any others.

"I'm going to open this box," I said finally, picking out a medium-sized box.

"Are you sure we should be opening any more of these?" Olivia asked.

Irrationally, I felt like I had a right to. Not saying anything, I pulled back the flaps to look inside. Packed right at the top was a CD. A Ray Charles CD.

"That's Amherst's," I said slowly. I reached a hand in and took the CD out. Looking at it, then at Olivia, I turned it over in my hands. "It's the Ray Charles Yun borrowed from Amherst."

There was a creak and we both looked up as the doors slid open to reveal Aunt Ung standing in the doorway. Obviously caught off guard, she looked at the two of us, sitting on the floor, surrounded by boxes, opened her mouth to say something, then closed it, the same way Yun used to.

"Is this all Yun's stuff?" I asked her, bluntly.

For a moment, there was a silence in the air. Then Aunt Ung nodded.

Everything was packed up neatly, a few books tied in a stack with string, a green and white scarf rolled up like a sleeping bag, a few old records still in their proper jacket envelopes. Everything was packed in so neatly. I stood up, CD still in hand, suddenly furious.

How could they leave me now, how could they of all people leave me?

"Why are you selling all your things?"

If she minded the harshness in my voice, she didn't flinch. I kept looking at Aunt Ung who returned my gaze with an almost serene expression. It now seemed obvious, the transformation she had made, from denial to tears, from despair to quiet determination. It now seemed obvious what she had wanted to say to me yesterday. She reached out to take my hand, angrily I snatched it back.

"Rachel, dear!" she said quietly. She reached for my hand again, holding it tightly between her palms.

"Aunt Ung, I need you to tell me why you're selling all your things", I said again, too loudly.

She looked down at my hand briefly, then she spoke calmly. As she spoke, the pieces came together and the sense of it all was like a lifting of a veil. She seemed so much more human in her moment's confession, so much more weak and tired. I am six again, then I am eighteen, twelve and twenty-six again. Standing with my hand in Aunt Ung's, it felt like I should be able to forgive her anything, curl up and eat her food, prepared with such tenderness; and believe it when she said it would be fine. I needed, wanted, needed her to tell me it would all be alright.

Then suddenly, two other women burst into the room, speaking to Aunt Ung in sharp, flowing voices without the slightest sign to acknowledge Olivia and me. With her hands crossed in front of her, Aunt Ung nodded towards the boxes. Copper and green, cold and uneven. Like clothes on a laundry line. I watched one of the women pass Aunt Ung and poke through them greedily, possessively, with no shame. From a slightly larger box, she removed a round object wrapped in newspaper. As she unwrapped it, I saw that it was one of the bronze bowls. There was more than one, the missing bowls were all there in the rest of the sealed boxes.

There was a sudden roaring in my ears, I had to leave the room, I couldn't witness this.

"I have to leave", I whispered.

Olivia bit her lip, looking first at Aunt Ung and then at me.

Rachel.

Her voice, normally like silver bells, stopped me in my tracks with its absoluteness.

We read his will tomorrow, Aunt Ung said, Yun's will.

He wrote a will? There was yet so much I seemed not to know.

Yes, she was gentler too, her wave of strength past. You will be there?

I could think of nothing I would rather do less. But of course.

"I'm going", I said, pushing through the door.

As I passed James Aimes and Josh, I saw that neither of them had moved, drinks in hand, faces almost dumb, rooted to the spot like they couldn't think of where else to go.

I am six again, then I am eighteen, twelve and twenty-six again. with nowhere to go.

A Painted Moment

Part Three
Without a shadow. Without a shore.

All I hear are whispers.

My feet swing even though I sit right on the edge of this too-tall chair, both arms flat on the wooden table top, elbows pointing outwards. Yun and I exchange glances but he says nothing, the fearful look in his eyes mirroring my own.

It's sunny today with a light breeze running through the trees, a mild late August day.

I have freckles on the tip of my nose and I'm a dark honey; next to Yun I look like a poster child for Coppertone, he who never tans, only turns a bright shade of lobster red and then pales again.

There is the sound of a door sliding and we both turn to look expectantly as they come down the stairs gingerly. Mum and Aunt Ung walk down the steps slowly, Mum with one arm around a subdued Chloe. Bringing up the rear is Olivia, holding a large bowl with both hands, careful to place each foot flat on the next step before lifting the back leg. We exchange glances again and Yun scoots over to my side to give the others room. Mum and Aunt Ung are talking in low voices above our heads, making sure Chloe is sat comfortably and the large bowl is transferred safely from Olivia's small hands to the centre of the table. Yun slides a wooden chopping-board covered with a thin dusting of flour and a slightly smaller bowl towards the others, careful to be unobtrusive, not sure if we're going to carry through our activity for the day, because it's something that we're unsure of.

"Thank you, children, for helping." Aunt Ung smiles around at all of us benignly, bringing her hands together, a jade bracelet sliding down towards her elbow with her slight movement. She has on an apron over one of her signature light green dresses and her hair is knotted tightly, high on her head.

"It is such a simple thing to make, *tang wan*, just watch what I do." She dips her hand into the large bowl, breaking off a small bit of white dough and deftly, with one hand, rolls it into a perfectly round ball and makes a slight indent with two fingers, like a dimple in the cheek. Then she takes up a silver spoon, dips it into the smaller bowl and measures out barely half a teaspoon of some red paste. She drops it into the shallow dent in the dough ball, then with that one hand again, closes the dough all around it so the red paste is concealed inside. White. Smooth. Perfect.

"There." She pops it onto the wooden chopping board. "*Tang wan* for the Moon Festival. We can have these tonight, after dinner, if we make enough, with crushed sugar and a ginger soup. We will want at least three for every person sitting around this table, not forgetting Uncle Ung, Rachel's father and Ang, who will eat at least five."

Yun opens his mouth to ask a question, then closes it, thinking better of it quickly. Mum sees this and with one hand on Chloe's shoulder, says:

"Chloe will be staying with us for a few days." She turns her eyes to Olivia. "And if you want, Oli – if you don't want to be by yourself – you're welcome to stay as well. We'll have more fun that way."

Chloe lowers her head so that her shoulder-length hair falls forward to cover the emerging purple bruise on her left cheek-bone. Anxiously, I look at my mum again, who shakes her head at me quickly, almost imperceptibly, I think. Olivia nods, quick to confirm the absence of her parents, nothing unusual there, wanting to stay with us. Aunt Ung breaks off a small ball of dough and passes it to Chloe, who, after a moment's hesitation, takes it with a small word of thanks. We all dig in, making *tang wan* of various sizes and differing success, Yun starting in on a story about animals in a forest, his dough balls becoming scrawny rabbits and giraffes with stumpy legs. Mum and Aunt Ung leave us to our own devices and settle down on the stairs, still talking just between themselves. Chloe cracks a smile as Olivia asks why Yun's horse looks like an ant-eater, but immediately, a hand goes to her cheek and her eyes redden in an instant. I kick Yun's legs under the table and he looks at me reproachfully, the ant-eater suspended in the air. I look significantly at Chloe. His forehead creases in concentration for a split second and then clears in a moment of clarity. He squashes the ant-eater, two rabbits and the stumpy giraffe into a big lump.

He then quickly breaks it up into four pieces with the very same deftness with which Aunt Ung makes perfect little *tang wan*; one is stretched long and thin, two are of average size and one is smaller and slight. Olivia and I watch curiously, balls half complete – Aunt Ung will eventually finish the dessert completing everything in half the time – as gradually, blobby figures appear.

"Chubs."

Chloe looks up at Yun. He puts the four figures in front of her.

"Oli." He points to one of the average-sized figures, with long hair and a crooked smile. "That's me." He points at the other average-sized figure, with huge biceps and a long neck. "The one like the daddy-long-legs is Rache." I scowl at him and Chloe can't help but giggle. "And that's you." He pushes the last one towards her, the smallest figure in a skirt. Inaudibly, he holds his breath, waiting to see how she will react. Olivia tries to resume making *tang wan*, with one eye surreptitiously still watching Chloe.

Aunt Ung gets up from the stairs, calling out to us that she'll return with some tea and some iced chocolate drinks.

A tiny butterfly comes to rest on the edge of the smaller bowl, attracted by the colour of the red bean paste; I watch its brilliant blue wings flutter in the wind, and try to imagine making a flute out of a blade of glass. Chloe takes the little figures, turning them over and over with a small smile.

She makes the figure of me dance, my long legs wobbling.

***

What looked like mist rose off the ground but it could be light spray from the rain that was spitting down. The drumming sound above my head on the porch roof was inconsistent. Pit. Pat. Pitter. I was stalling, hunched into myself against the chill, hesitating on the porch. Beyond the door there must already be a few people – Glory and Josh surely, perhaps James Aimes.

I had been torn between dread of coming over again and dread of staying in my house any longer. In the end, I had chosen to leave the house to stand on this porch for as long as I could bear.

Glancing over my shoulder, I spied Olivia coming through the woods, the collar of her coat pulled up, her long golden hair loose around her face.

It had been an almost entirely silent morning. Chloe had made breakfast but very early, so there'd been no need for her to sit with us while we ate. She had retreated as soon as Olivia and I had emerged from our rooms; but as we sat at the dining-table, I had been preoccupied. It was as if I could hear the abject, lip pressing silence, somewhere in the house, emanating forcefully.

And this morning, it appeared Olivia didn't have any energy to speak, all of it sapped after a long and strained conversation with Will, not been entirely muffled by the walls of the house.

So we sat and picked over our food in silence. I was staring off into space, probably chewing a bit of hair when the doorbell rang. I glanced blankly at the door.

"Expecting someone?" Olivia asked.

I shook my head, getting up and crossing out of the kitchen to the living-room. Even before I opened the door, I could see the blurry outline through the thickened glass.

"Morning."

Sylvain stomped his feet and grinned at me sheepishly.

"Morning Rache, sorry to bother you so early," he said, "Did you just wake up?"

"No, no," I ran a hand through my tangled hair, "Just slow moving this morning."

I beckoned him in and he stepped through lightly.

"Here to speak to Chloe?"

He nodded, shrugging out of his jacket.

"Did you take her home last night?" I asked, padding off.

"Yeah, it was pretty late. Did we wake you?"

I didn't answer him as I headed off to look for Chloe. When I told her he was here, a look I didn't recognize crossed her face. It wasn't surprise, it wasn't pleasure but I would say it wasn't displeasure.

Chloe and Sylvain moved out onto the back porch, shutting the glass doors firmly behind them. Chloe settled beneath a blanket in a low reclining chair while Sylvain stood leaning against a pillar, his hands in his pockets, head down. From the turn of Chloe's head, I couldn't tell if she was looking at him or not; hard to guess the mood.

They didn't seem to mind that they had an audience but I minded. Olivia remained unmoved in her seat at the dining-table, while I stood there, unsure what I should do. I cleared the plates, washed up quickly and then turned to look at Olivia again. She was still in the same position.

"Oli?"

She looked up at me, her face drawn.

"Are you...is Will?"

She shook her head, crossing her arms.

"Nothing's happened", she answered. "Everything is still the same."

I nodded uncertainly, and then said that I was going to head over to Aunt Ung's first. But as I slowly got dressed in my room, I realized that that wasn't really where I wanted to be either. As the sweater went over my head, I thought a walk might be the thing.

I let the cold, late morning air have me. Under mournful trees and the grey sky, I walked in enough circles for the water in the ground to dampen the ends of my jeans before I finally gave up and headed for the Ung's. And so here I stood as Oli approached. I waited while she scraped her shoes delicately on the edge of the step.

"Shall we?" She didn't question why I was standing there, not going in.

Resignedly, I nodded as she pulled the long bell-cord. Behind the door, I heard uncertain footsteps and then it was Glory who pulled open the door.

"Are we very late?" Olivia asked as Glory let us in. Our shoes came off but there were no slippers to be had in their stead.

Glory shook her head.

"I don't think so. We're still...well I guess we're still waiting," Glory said ruefully, "Actually I'm not entirely sure what it is we're waiting for. Where's Chubs?"

Neither of us said anything as we followed closely behind into the sitting room where the others stood. There was no sign of

Aunt Ung but my eyes passed over a man who sat on the sofa, a briefcase lying flat on his lap, secure. His eyes were darting around nervously.

I moved to the windows facing the sitting room and stared out, though the windows were slightly fogged. I didn't want to face the others this morning. My head hurt. Behind me, James Aimes shifted impatiently. I wished desperately that he would keep still.

I wasn't sure for how long we all stood there. I think at some point, Chloe and Sylvain let themselves in and came into the room. There was throat-clearing and someone with a glass sipped noisily.

Then came Aunt Ung's wind-chime voice.

"*Lai*", she said. "Come sit."

Slowly, I turned and so we were gathered, while above our heads, white paper mobiles tinkled, in slowly circular patterns. Aunt Ung went to sit on the edge of the sofa with her head turned slightly away, her hands held tightly in her lap. We arranged ourselves amongst the stiff-backed chairs and the low settees on which the silk-covered cushions would slide left and right, and the air settled uncomfortably in our midst, in the gaps between our bodies, while outside the frost hung in the air. The early morning light was weak and seemed barely to infiltrate the trees and the windows of the house. The man put his hands flat on the top of his briefcase, then thinking better of it, removed his hands. In the rooms beyond, Uncle Ung hovered, unseen but felt.

We were quiet, in our gathering.

I sat, furthest away from both Aunt Ung and the man, on an ottoman at the back of the room. I looked at the backs of everyone's heads, I looked at the floor, I tried very hard not to look at Aunt Ung and her determination to be strong.

I so did not want to be here and yet, I did.

And what I wanted was to hear what Yun had written so secretly that even I had not known nor had access to it. For a moment, there might have even been excitement, excitement seething underneath my layer of stunned pain, that there was a side of Yun that I was to know for the first time.

What would I hear?

A Painted Moment

The man stood up.

'Thank you, thank you for coming", the man said, looking around at us earnestly.

Finally, I realized that this was the man from the funeral and I stared at him. The man cleared his throat, touched his fingers to his temple. Why was he here? He glanced at Aunt Ung, who looked up at all of us, and there was a glimmer of her former self, a self that would have been imperious without that benign lift at the tip of her lips.

"Thank you for coming", Aunt Ung echoed and her hand went out to indicate to the man, gracefully, that he should continue. Quickly, he bent down, opened the briefcase and removed a piece of paper. Snapping the briefcase shut, he clutched at it nervously before straightening up again. The man cleared his throat again and looked at us.

"This is…what I am about to read…is…unusual. I have been instructed to dispense with the formalities and speak, as it were… that is to say…" – He touched his fingertips to his temple again. – "It is…informal and please excuse me. – I don't know you all…."

His voice trailed away and he looked down at his sheet of paper.

Even through this man's voice – squeaky, like a mouse – always emphasizing the wrong words, mispronouncing them and rushing in his eagerness to finish, there would be words and wishes from Yun in this space between our bodies.

For a brief moment. At least.

"To start and to end in much the same way, to touch on what I know of and what I wish for all of you:

To Sylvain. I leave our *die xien* and an old hammer, so you can decide what you want to do with either or neither or both.

To Aimes. I leave my collection of comics, their worth in cash less than their worth in memories.

To Amherst, I return your Ray Charles finally and thank you because I can only say that his music opened new doors for me where I didn't know there were walls.

To Glory and Josh, I leave my saplings planted in the front garden because they need to be taken care of, and loved and brought up in a home that is a real home. Because even plants need love. Let alone humans. And each other.
To Chloe, I also leave our *die xien* and an old hammer, so you can fight over what to do with either or neither or both.
To Oli, I leave patience and the books in my library, may these things bring you the peace that you seek.
To my parents, you know what I have left you and I hope you know what you've left me with too. I hope to carry it with me no matter where I am headed.

I could say that I want you all to live long and prosper. Be happy and don't grieve. But what I really want to say is, I enjoyed it and you, and you and me together. Thank you for sharing it with me. That's it. Now live long and prosper."

And that was all.
That fragment of Yun that lingered in the air slowly dissipated with those last words.
The man looked around, embarrassed it seemed, the job that was normally a lawyer's to do, passed on to this uneasy, nervous man. He replaced the piece of paper within the large confines of the briefcase and gestured to a box at his feet that presumably contained the contents of what Yun had left in his will but no one moved forward to claim anything. After what seemed another long while, Aunt Ung stood up and ushered the man out of the room, speaking in unhurried undertones, probably offering him tea in the next room as the rest of us were left with each other.
The air in the room had changed.
His words had unsettled us all, in true Yun fashion, in an almost comical way. But they had also cleaned the air a little, rinsed out the mustiness that had settled on everyone in the time we had gathered, perhaps ever since they had returned to the island.
There was no real reason for this. But somehow, the change was almost palpable.

Amherst was the first to get up and go to the box. He bent over awkwardly, put his hand in and came up with the Ray Charles CD, turned it over in his hand and then returned to his seat on the sofa. He was unruffled and almost thoughtful as he closed his eyes, leaning his head back. A low humming, thrumming seemed to come from the back of his throat.

James Aimes sought out the next box, heaved it into his arms and took it aside to look through the contents on his own in a corner. His expression was perplexed as if he didn't quite understand what Yun had said, and I thought that it would probably be up to Sylvain to explain it to him, as he always seemed to do when people left the room.

Josh and Glory, after a short whisper stood up too.

"We're going to go check out those saplings", Josh said simply, to the room at large; and they left the room, hand in hand, the space between them close.

Sylvain loped forward and dug through the first box till he came upon a small plastic box, inside of which was the *die xien*. He tossed it up in the air and caught it again, a strange grin on his face. He glanced up at Chloe, made a motion with his head and they too left the room.

And then there was nothing but silence, the silence of people thinking hard thoughts. Olivia, to my right and slightly ahead of me, looked down at her hands, shaking her head almost imperceptibly from time to time.

The fact that Yun had had no words for me slowly settled like a parachute billowed out on a grass field.

What would I do now?

I found that I wanted to leave too. I wanted to leave the room because I was the only one Yun had not left a message for. The side of him that I had wanted to know, the secrets that I had wanted to learn, the last of him that I had wanted to clutch to my chest and crush till there was no air left – they never existed and the promise of that dissipated with the last of his words.

I stood up. My sudden movement made Olivia start.

"I…" I looked at her, my words lost.

"Are you leaving?" There was a tightening around her tired eyes.

And even though I wanted to say that I was, I didn't, because there was no where for me to go.

"Don't leave", Olivia said.

I didn't move.

"I just, I need a moment," Olivia said to me, "With you here."

I heard panic edge her voice, a panic that was never usually there in her voice, her usual voice that was like liquid honey.

I sat back down on my ottoman. There was nowhere I wanted to go in particular. Anyway.

I had been hollowed out and I was afraid of what the emptiness of the house would do to me.

"Oli", I said.

She shook her head, her hand shifting in my direction slightly.

So I closed my mouth and remained in my seat for moments that stretched out. In the room, there was an emptiness and Amherst's low, soft humming.

Hours, days later, it could have been minutes later, the lightest of footsteps

"Rachel."

I looked up unwillingly. Aunt Ung stood in the doorway out to the corridor, without the man. Her hands clasped in front of her, she looked at me for a moment before saying quietly.

"I think we may need some help organizing some items, please. Would you mind?"

Inwardly, I flinched, repulsed by her words. On the outside, I held her level gaze. Behind her, I could see that some of the others who had left the room earlier were now bustling. I could also discern Sylvain's thumping tread from above my head.

There was nothing for it. I nodded and both Olivia and I got up to follow her through to the adjoining room.

All around us were boxes, books and plates, candles, checkers and photo-frames.

Aunt Ung gestured at Glory who came in to take over, while she herself flitted quickly away like she couldn't bear to watch us.

I sat on the rug, legs tucked under me and cast about. Glory had quickly started to make herself useful by stacking loose sheets of newspaper and bubble wrap by our side while she moved off to check on some of the price-tagging. Somewhere, someone had Aunt Ung's list of items – which part of their lives they were leaving behind and which they were taking with them. I reached over and squeezed a bubble between my thumb and forefinger and felt the satisfying snap.

Glory and Olivia conferred briefly before Olivia picked up two bags and a flattened cardboard box.

"Addictive", Olivia said, unloading the lot and plopping down next to me. I squeezed another but this one fizzled out flatly. The activity seemed to have brought her back to life, and the warmth in her voice returned.

"Here", Olivia said, pushing one of the bags towards me, "We're wrapping the chopsticks and spoons in newspaper and putting them in a box."

I looked in the bag.

"That's going to take hours", I said.

Olivia had popped open the cardboard box and was folding over the flaps so it would hold its shape.

"Yes, I'm sure it will", she responded.

I was being churlish, I realized, but I didn't know what to do with that particular emotion. I took a sheet of newspaper, put one hand into the bag, pulled out a chopstick, folded the edge of the newspaper over it, rolled the chopstick over once; I then took another chopstick, lined it up and rolled the whole thing over once more. In the newspaper under the chopsticks, there was an ad seeking an English tutor for a child in Primary Five.

"Hey", I observed, "A few weeks back and you could've applied to be an English tutor."

Olivia looked up from masking the box.

"How old is that paper?" she asked, amused.

"Just last month."

"Oh." She sealed the edge of the box, flipped it over and then scooted over to the bags with the chopsticks.

"Apparently, we had record sunshine that month", I went on, turning the paper over.

Olivia laughed, and grabbed my chopsticks playfully. They fell to the rug and I had to start all over again.

"I don't need sun. I would settle for no rain right now", I said, looking out of the windows as Glory passed by again, doling out more newspapers, absent-mindedly wiping her hands on her jeans, scurrying off to another room. From somewhere in the house, I could hear Sylvain's voice, the words inaudible, and then surprisingly, Chloe's laugh. The sound warmed me without warning and I blinked, trying to comprehend the feeling. It had been a while since I had felt anything close to this.

The churlishness passed.

"What do you think of what Yun said?"

I glanced back at Olivia, who was looking at me now. Her eyes were unreadable, her face impassive.

'What do I think?"

"I wonder what he meant. That I should be more patient. Have I been impatient?"

I shook my head, she had never been.

"So what did he mean?" She looked down at the newspaper she was holding. "Oh, Amherst made the papers. Junior High interview." She held it up, rustled it, put it back down in her lap, her eyes scanning some of the other columns. Inaudibly, almost, she caught her breath.

I kept wrapping chopsticks.

"Maybe he meant with Chubs."

To her credit, she did not flinch when I said it, which made me think she already knew what conclusion I would arrive at.

"Yes. Funny that." Olivia sighed. "Patience, for years, patience."

I didn't know what to say, looked down at my papers.

"Local deer, endangered", I quipped.

"I don't know what to be patient for", Olivia said. "I don't even know who's forgiving whom at this point. I don't even think it's forgiveness I need. Did I really wrong her that badly?"

Again, I said nothing.

"I know you don't want to take sides. But I didn't know about Will. She never said anything."

"It's not just Will."

"Then what? The scholarship?"

"She had to fight too hard for everything. And you never had to."

"I worked hard."

"She fought though. And yet."

"And yet what?"

"You were the one who found happiness."

"And so I don't deserve this baby?"

"Oli, she didn't mean it. She would never mean that."

Olivia's eyes narrowed hurtfully for a moment.

"I would have taken her for someone who never said anything she didn't mean", Olivia said.

I shook my head.

"She has pride."

"As do I."

"Oli", I breathed softly.

Olivia put her fingers to the bridge of her nose, again the tightening. Then, suddenly, she thrust her newspaper at me. I didn't understand the gesture. Without opening her eyes, she said.

"Read that."

I looked down at the article, realizing it was yesterday's paper. I looked through it, not sure what I was looking for and then found that in front of me was the article I had scanned without really reading. Scandal. I read it now, slowly, and when I was finished, I read it again.

I looked at Olivia.

Her face was dark and sad, and there was remorse.

"I could say that's not working hard," Olivia said, in a voice that should have been caustic but wasn't.

"You wouldn't though."

"No," she replied, needlessly. "What I will say is that that shouldn't have happened."

"The...his...wife found out?"

"Who else? But you don't fire someone for something you had a part in. What a bastard!" The last, with vehemence.

"She couldn't have known", I answered softly, on Chloe's behalf.
There was a brief pause.
"Could she?"
"Why do you think, then?"
Our conversation from yesterday came back to me. Was it love?
Olivia shrugged and then regarded me for another moment.
"I thought you should know the details", she said. "Maybe I
shouldn't have told you, or been the one to tell you. But Chloe
should have said something."
"I would have wanted Chubs to tell me," I said firmly. "No
matter what's happened. She wouldn't have. She would never."
And then Olivia stopped, looking beyond me, before she turned
back to the chopsticks.
My heart skipped a beat.
I turned to see Chloe and Sylvain behind me, laden with books.
The one time I was loud, she had heard me.
"Chubs."
Chloe was preternaturally calm. She watched Olivia turn
chopsticks over in newspaper, then looked at me.
I cringed, waiting for an explosion.
"I should have said something", she echoed, to our surprise.
She put down the books and asked Sylvain if he wanted to get
some air. Sylvain set his little stack down, dusted his hands, and
they left quietly.
I turned back around and noticed that Olivia had stopped
wrapping. Her long slender hands were…trembling?
Maybe she shouldn't have told me.
The warm feeling in my chest was gone. So there was nothing for
it but to keep wrapping.

***

"Hello? That wasn't the response I'd expected." Olivia's voice is
slightly bemused though far away, the line to Paris slightly shaky.
"I know I'm far away, but I couldn't help it. I had to call you.
Rachel? Rachel Glass? Are you still there?"

Paris feels very far away, over a dodgy connection and across time zones. Olivia feels very far away from where I am frozen momentarily.

"I'm sorry, I'm sorry, Oli. That's great news!" One hand at my chest, I rush in belatedly with my, "Congratulations. I can't believe it."

Yun freezes, his big eyes round, a coffee-mug half way to his mouth. He's leaning back in a chair, one leg propped up against a bench tucked neatly under the wooden table. We've been talking and the call had interrupted our casual discourse this afternoon.

Oli? He mouths. I nod, my fingers pinching tightly at the bridge of my nose, pressure round my head.

Over the crackle of the line, I imagine I can smell the scent of strawberries.

"Rache?"

"Sorry, yes, I'm here."

"I know, I'm a little shocked myself, in fact more than a little I think," Olivia rattles on, the sound of muffled music in the background, maybe running water. "He caught me completely off guard."

"Of course you were." – My senses were coming back to me quickly now. – "How were you to know? ... Oli, where are you? I can't really hear you." I make flapping gestures at Yun as I pace the coffee-shop floor, my candy-coloured flip-flops slapping loudly against the wood. He springs to his feet and tries to put his ear to the phone but I am moving too erratically for him to follow me properly.

"Running a bath and waiting for Will in our hotel room, he's gone out to buy some flowers I think. I had to call you straight away. Rache – he said the most soulful things I've ever heard. Not some corny line from a movie, nothing that prosaic." She paused searching for words, "I don't know what I felt that moment, I felt...I felt like I was drowning."

"Drowning?" I echo, "Surely that's not a good feeling."

"No, no! – Drowning? That's not what I meant. – I was breathless. He left me completely breathless. There was nothing but the stars, the dark sky, the breeze, him and me. Breathless." She tries the word out again with a certain sense of satisfaction, "After that there was no other way but to say yes."

"No other way...."

"I know it's only been nine months, but these nine months have been...they've just been breathtaking."

"Oli, are you sure?"

"Sure about him?"

"Yes, well as you say, it's only been nine months", I reason, "You're so young."

"Yes I know, but there was really no other way, Rache, you need to have heard him to understand!"

Feeling slightly weak, I listen to Olivia as she continues on about the wedding, the invitations, the dress. Until finally, she pauses and asks if something is the matter. Not at all, I'm so happy for you. You don't really sound it, Olivia responds slowly.

I bite my lip, searching for courage to ask that question, but falter. "No, of course I'm happy for you, Oli!" I nod firmly, even as Yun watches me over the coffee-mug again.

"Rache, if there's anything – oh I think that's Will at the door. Listen, let's talk another time, alright sweetheart? Take care, say hi to Yun."

"Oli – "

"I'll call you back, Rache, bye!"

And then the line goes dead. I put down my mobile phone and look at Yun blankly. He spreads his hands, an eyebrow cocked, ready for what I have report.

"She's engaged!" I say lamely.

"To whom?" Yun asks, not too much incredulity on his face.

"William", I say pointedly, "Will."

"Will? Will?...Oh...*that* Will!"

"*That* Will!" I confirm.

We both look at each other – mine is a sense of helpless foreboding. I am sure Yun has thoughts that he has yet to share. At the back of my mind, I am all too aware that Chloe and Glory will walk through the door at any moment, arms laden with late summer fruit. Behind that thought is another image of Olivia, her arms held away from her body, standing on the edge of the river bank, her body tilting forward into the black night.

"Are we going to tell her?" I ask a little plaintively.

"Chubs?"

"Yeah."

"Would you rather she found out from someone else?" Yun asks me, returning to his coffee; the very contours of his face the picture of rhetoric. Ofcourse I don't want Chloe to find out from someone else, but I also do not relish being the one to break the news. I sit down on the bench and push his feet off. He grumbles and then meets my gaze, leaning over to squeeze my arm reassuringly. Of course we have to tell her. And we probably should tell Olivia not to bother sending her an invitation.

He's right, as always.

I look out of the window at the waning sun that makes long crossed shadows along the floor, the sky is still a high, brilliant blue. For now, there is peace and somewhere, hope. I want to savour this and not have to think about telling Chloe. Then there is a creak at the door, the tinkle of a carefree bell, someone laughs giddily in the doorway and I turn my head to greet them.

***

We were all squashed in Josh's mini, we shouldn't have been because we had all been drinking, but we were all in the car.

Our day had worn itself out, in our quiet packing.

Sylvain and Chloe had not returned, and then Aunt Ung had insisted we have dinner at her place, so we stayed to eat a simple meal, also quiet, while we drank *shochu*. It could have been a scene from so many other nights, us around their large table in their kitchen, eating rice with eggs and tomatoes, *tofu* with *hou tou gu*, the ends of our chopsticks clicking against one another's. Simple, just like any other night.

And then Aunt Ung had retired and the boys suggested heading out for a spin.

And somehow we had ended up here.

Josh pulled the mini in to park a little aggressively, and turned off the ignition as we all piled out, making our way a little unsteadily up the side of the hill, in the dark, towards the cemetery and the big tree. The wind whipped.

Had I been slightly less tipsy, I would have questioned the wisdom of Olivia climbing the fairly steep incline, in the dark, but as it was, she was climbing quicker than me, ahead, focused it seemed. In my youth, I had suffered many a scraped palm and knee, many a banged head running up and down this steep slope and that was in my fearless time. Again I tried to remember how we had ended up here, but as always, it seemed there was no reason for the general decision that was made. We just made it and then followed it, like lemmings, as we had always done.

Clumsily and breathlessly, I finally joined the group at the top, where they had settled variously on the different gravestones, as if they were deck-chairs. Up here, what was light drizzle by now was being tossed up by the wind to form mist, and I shivered. Not wanting to get the seat of my jeans wet, I too sought out a cold slab of marble to park my bottom on. Bottles were pulled out and thrust into the soft ground.

Somewhere a lighter flicked and there was the barely perceptible crackle of paper, and then the end of a joint was stoked. A torch flicked on. Glory. Then another. Amherst.

"Are you ...?" I was incredulous.

"Yes", Olivia said throatily, holding her breath, before letting out a cloud of smoke. "Yes, we are."

"Thanks to good old Amherst", James Aimes smirked.

Amherst hummed lightly.

A slight smile threatened to tip the edges of my lips.

"Do you still get high?" I asked, as Josh passed Glory a whisky bottle.

"There wasn't anything to do and it wasn't like we fucking wanted to speak to anyone anyway", James Aimes said dismissively. "And then Amherst here came up with a plan."

He stretched languorously with a contented sigh, as if he wasn't lying on someone's gravestone.

"Would you like some?" Josh asked, holding it out to me, burning tip away from me.

I shook my head, reaching out for the whisky bottle instead.

"Anyway, so like I was saying – why shouldn't you? Why the fuck not?"

Josh shifted uncomfortably through his haze of cloudy comfort.

"Well for one, I don't think we have – well that is, I don't think we have – that sort of money saved away yet," Josh explained thickly, "And I don't think Glory would want to anyway."

James Aimes snorted derisively.

"Come on, you wimp, does it really matter whether Glory wants to? She doesn't understand the importance of growth – how could she?" James Aimes punctuated his sentence with sharp stabs, joint held tightly between two fingers, adding darkly, "Mark my words, women never want growth, they want stability. Stability. That's what it's all about."

Glory got up, kicked James Aimes, and went back to her gravestone. I stared at James Aimes, speechless, as he continued to eulogize along similar lines.

"You're no Superman yourself, you know."

James Aimes looked at me in surprise.

"What?"

"I said you're no Superman yourself. Don't tell him how or how not to care about Glory!" I didn't realize I still had the ability to surprise even myself. He looked at me with his mouth slightly open, like a goldfish.

Glory giggled. And in my heart of hearts, I was smug.

James Aimes clamped his mouth shut.

"If you could be any superhero, who would you be?" Josh asked suddenly, his mind off on another tangent already. There was an abrupt silence as everyone seemed caught up in this question and contemplated it in all seriousness.

"I would be that blue and green woman – the one with the red hair – from *X-Men*", I answered, pre-empting the others to select a role first. "…What was her name?"

"Mystique! She's not a superhero! The X-Men are mutants, not superheroes", Josh objected.

"Why would you want to be Mystique?" James Aimes asked, almost derisive, ignoring Josh.

"Then I could become anyone I wanted, chameleon-like." My voice was slightly defensive, still riled in the wake of his comments about Glory.

"Mystique," Amherst repeated, almost dreamy, "What about Spiderman?" Before anyone could question him, he asked if Transformers were considered superheroes.

"I don't like the crawling thing with Spiderman", James Aimes said critically.

"He doesn't crawl", Amherst explained patiently.

"I'd be The Hulk", James Aimes announced loudly with another stretch, "The Hulk would crush Spiderman."

"The Hulk is an out-of-control mistake", Amherst said haughtily, rocking back and forth on the balls of his feet.

"So is Spiderman", James Aimes countered nastily.

"Aren't they all freaks of some sort?" Josh broke in, laughing a little.

"Why d'you ask the question then, dumb-ass?" James Aimes flopped back, ash falling from the tip of the joint.

Josh shrugged. Typical.

"What about you, Oli?" I peered at her closely.

"Speaking of *X-Men*, you remind me of Jean Grey, Oli." James Aimes voice was far away.

"Which one was Jean Grey?"

"The mind-reading chick."

"That sounds pretty decent."

"I wouldn't want to read minds", Olivia said suddenly, sharp. Olivia would rather not know what other people thought of her, quietly continuing blindly on in the prospect of mutually agreed deceit and assumptions. Amherst began to hum under his breath again.

The joint was passed to Olivia. One drag. Two. She passed it on to Glory who held it uncertainly.

I was so very tired. Maybe the smoke in the air was getting to me as well. Had it really been that long since I had cut loose and tried to have some fun.

The others continued to squabble but Olivia was quiet. I pivoted towards her as far as the angle where I sat would allow; she was actually perched on the edge of large rock.

"What's up, Oli?" I asked, under my breath, "Are you alright? Maybe you've had enough."

Olivia tossed her hair slightly.

"I'm fine", she answered, softly.

"It can't be good for you," I said pointedly. "This – and the drinking – it can't be good for you."

In the background, Amherst continued to hum, and the conversation shifted again as Josh and James Aimes droned on about expanding the coffee shop.

Olivia shook her head, almost holding her breath, and in the dragged out quiet, I waited for what she seemed on the cusp of saying.

"She's right, I don't deserve this child."

I stared at Olivia blankly, uncomprehending for a moment, those moments of expectation curtailing my understanding.

"What do you mean?" I asked. Olivia repeated herself patiently.

"Don't say that!" I said sharply; and Amherst stopped humming. "She didn't mean it."

"It doesn't matter whether she meant it or not", Olivia replied. Her voice was still too patient. I was at a loss what to say next, lost in my confusion what she might be thinking, or what was going through her mind. Had the obscured moon been any brighter, I might have been able to read the expression in her eyes.

"I believe Chet Baker's greatest album to be...", Amherst started loudly and out of the blue; then stopped. "I don't know which album I consider the best actually. I'm torn, torn between *The Italian Sessions* and *The Quintet* Album – yes, *The Quintet* Albums."

Josh and James Aimes stopped talking for a moment to regard Amherst foggily.

"Who?" Josh squinted.

"Does it matter, man? He's dead. And who listens to that kind of dead-beat, poncy old music when they're not stoned, anyway?"

James Aimes said wheezily, propped up on two elbows now, his head rolling from side to side.

Amherst clapped a hand to his chest, injured, and I gave James Aimes's leg a hearty slap.

"Ow – what the – alright, it's not poncy, but come on, A, you don't mean to say it impresses the girls?" James Aimes looked at him plaintively, almost sincere in his state and Josh guffawed.

"If you haven't noticed, James, I'm not actually interested in what some people deem to be the gentler sex", Amherst said stiffly.

Josh burst out laughing and it was James Aimes's turn to squint through the smoke. In spite of myself, I wanted to suppress a smile at his revelation, only ten years after leaving secondary school, when, out of the corner of my eye, I realized that Olivia was staring into space, obviously not listening.

A scene came back to me. High summer. The air heavy with the smell of strawberries, a lofty breeze catching the scent and teasing it through our hair. Above these gravestones, this little cemetery, this old, old tree, our kites flew high in the air, running with the clouds.

I wanted that feeling, wanted to see those red and blue squares like cut-outs across the sky. Not this blackness without stars. There was something in her face that made me suddenly afraid. I heard James Aimes ask Amherst what he meant as I inched closer to Olivia.

Suddenly, with a yelp, James Aimes tossed the whisky bottle up and it flew through the air before hitting the ground and rolling rapidly away.

"Don't brood over what she said," I whispered urgently, leaning in towards her, "She wasn't thinking straight."

"But that's exactly it", Olivia answered. "I think she's right."

Our faces were so close, I imagined the light gold freckles in her eyes could have danced for me.

"Now is not the time to be making decisions about what's wrong and right". I gripped her arm.

Then Olivia loosened my grip on her arm, and as a fresh bottle was passed around, she stood and moved slowly away, picking a route round the headstones, around Josh and Amherst.
My brow furrowed.
"Is she alright?" Glory asked me, near.
I shook my head.
She was quiet for a moment, and then.
"Drink?" Glory asked, heavily.
"No, I've had a lot, thanks", I answered, pushing the bottle away.
"I never see you drink any more", Glory commented.
"And I don't usually see you drink this much."
We stared at each other glumly before I surprised myself again.
"I wish Yun were here."
The words hung out there and I realized it was the first time I had said aloud these very words that I seemed to want the most. If Yun were here, he would know what to say to Oli, would know where to find Chubs. He would know and be able to talk to them, make them laugh, show them the way. He would know. He would make everything better.
Glory reached out to put a hand on my arm and my insides twisted viciously.
He always did.
"Oli?" It was Amherst.
I turned quickly and saw the shadow of Olivia swaying in the slight distance, ominously. Then she dropped away with a soft cry.
Strawberries.
I was onto my feet, even as the boys grappled in confusion.
Grabbing Glory's torch, I picked my way through the half dark, inched my way down the slope, skidding, careful. Josh managed to overtake me and we both saw a darkened crumple ahead, and then he was kneeling beside her, calling uncertainly.

I see her walking towards me fast, her long golden hair catching the light as it streams behind her. She is waving a thick book in her hand triumphantly, the edges of the pages gilded in gold. You have to love me for this, it's perfect, she crows. Her eyes are shining and she pulls at a book-mark, opening the book and placing it triumphantly on the table in front of me. Chloe peers curiously at the page. The Bible? Chloe asks incredulously. Behind me, Yun swears as he almost topples from a ladder he's up, trying to reach an impossibly high book-shelf. *Three Wisemen*, she answers excitedly, we all come bearing gifts, it's perfect for the book-store, everyone looks for that perfect something.

I gave James Aimes the torch and knelt down, pushing Josh away, from where he was trying to prop up Olivia's limp body. I tried to gather her towards me, pushing her hair from her face and I realized how light she was. We all come bearing gifts.

***

Our faces, when reflected, are different. Left is right and right is left and curiously we are recognizable but still different. The faucet on the second sink from the right is faulty and drips sporadically. Chloe is calmly brushing at her curls with her fingers but her lips are pursed and I don't know if I want to say anything, so I hug my books to my chest and lean against the cold tiled wall. My bangs are tickling my eyes, and I puff out a breath so they lift and then settle back in the same place. The door opens and then Olivia walks in, slightly breathless. Chloe glances at her in the mirror and if possible, her lips press further together.

"There you are!" Olivia says brightly, "Yun told me to come in here and look. We're going for a drink, come with us."

I push myself off the wall and stand there awkwardly, shifting my weight, feeling like if I move either way I will betray one of them.

"You two go ahead", Chloe said stiffly, more for my benefit than for Olivia's, continuing to arrange her short hair.

Olivia comes forward till she is standing next to Chloe, putting her long slender hands on the edge of the sink.

"Chubs, is something the matter? You seem – different lately", Olivia asks gently.

Chloe looks through her bag almost ostentatiously and fishes out some lip gloss. She leans forward so she's closer to the mirror, removes the cap and squeezes a small amount onto her lips.

"Chubs?"

"Don't call me that", Chloe answers evenly, smacking her lips and turning her head to check her application. Olivia could have been a fly on the wall to her.

"Chloe, then! Talk to me!"

Chloe takes a finger and rubs her upper lip very gently.

"You can't keep doing this forever, you have to tell me what the matter is."

Chloe stops rubbing and their eyes meet in the mirror. Their faces, reflected in this instant, look so similar, all gold and tawny and blonde. Their arms are golden from the beginnings of a warm summer and they are both on the leaner side of their ideal weight. They are, in this instant, interchangeable. Behind them, I can fade in the shadows, with my darker skin and long dark-brown hair. I almost want to.

"I can, actually. Not talk to you forever. Quite easily," Chloe says deliberately.

Olivia stands there, very still, her long, tawny eyes on Chloe. Then I watch as she wheels away from her and indicates to me that she will wait outside before leaving as quickly as she came. In her wake, there is a defiant silence.

"It's not her fault", I finally say, my voice small but determined, "She wanted this as much as you." I am not sure that speaking to Chloe about it is the right approach, but it suddenly feels like I have to stand up for Olivia.

"It's not my first concern, whether it's her fault or not", Chloe answers, her eyes on me now, "And yes, I know she wanted it."

I know she knows. Chloe is one of the most insightful people I know. But I am not and I don't understand. My face as usual, betrays me. Chloe puts away her make-up bag and turns to face me. Her eyes are unusually bright and I think I imagine a catch in her clear voice.

"She wanted it, Rache, but she didn't need it." Implicit there is that Chloe needs it. "She probably doesn't even know why she wanted it in the first place."

"But she would never do anything to hurt you intentionally", I say, so certain of Olivia's loyalty.

Chloe regards me sadly and maybe the expression on her face hardens.

"That's exactly it", she says bitterly. "She never does any of these things intentionally. We never hurt anyone we love intentionally."

She swings the bag over her shoulder and then straightens up before leaving the bathroom, leaving just me and my lonely reflection in the mirror.

***

Waiting is a horrible thing.

Like a suspension of breath, what a relief when your lungs collapse and you draw in air so it expands again. I waited, holding Olivia close to me, as the others frantically dialled for the ambulance. I waited in the ambulance with Olivia, holding her hand as we sped to the hospital. I waited in the waiting room, alone, after explaining in hurried tones to those nurses who would listen that Olivia was pregnant and it was important, terribly important that they remember that. I left a message on Will's voicemail box and then sat in the waiting room, waiting some more. I remembered that time went by quicker if you kept your eyes away from the clock that hung on the pale green wall, I learnt that the last time waiting for Yun. Finally, I could stand it no longer, so I headed outside where a door next to the cafeteria led to a small sheltered corridor that overlooked the hospital gardens, ringed by pine trees. I sat, hunched, elbows on my knees, needing to hug myself, rocking back and forth. Mercifully, the wind whistling through the pines seem to be less ferocious and the biting cold more bearable. Please. Please.

"Rachel, dear."

I didn't question how she found me.

"Hi, Aunt Ung."

A Painted Moment

Aunt Ung came and sat next to me in the most languid and reassuring manner possible. Her shoes were soaked but she was still the most elegant woman I knew.

"How much longer? Do you know?" she asked quietly.

I shook my head.

"I'm not sure....They won't tell me....Even if they did, I'd hardly understand..."

I found I couldn't seem to focus long enough to put the sentence together, I was so tired.

"The other children, I told them to wait till the worst of the rain is over before coming over."

At another time, I might have smiled at the idea that to some of our elders, we would forever be children, never growing up, frozen in time. Now I would give anything for us all to be six again.

"That's a good idea", I managed eventually, leaning back.

"I am sure Olivia will pull through. Children, your bodies are like *mochi*, you can be constantly remoulded", Aunt Ung said to me, "The heart though; not so easy to remould. Like yours. I worry about yours."

If the words surprised me, they took more than a moment to register. I looked at her wordlessly.

"You have not been alright", she said simply. "You try. I see you try. It has been difficult, I understand that. Your heart aches and your body is tired. Sometimes, it is difficult living the same life again when actually it is no longer the same. But people still persist in believing it possible." Possibilities, there it was again. Her kind words dredged up the guilt I felt. I started to make an excuse for the way I had spoke to her earlier but she wouldn't let me.

"I wanted to tell you that we were leaving. Earlier, much earlier. But Yun told us to keep quiet about it. In his instructions, he told Uncle Ung and me to try and carry out his wishes without alerting you."

And yet, again. He had left me no instructions.

"I have to confess, I may not understand this completely, so it is my guess, my guess completely, but perhaps he thought you would try and stop us from leaving." She turned her gentle eyes toward me, as if to say, it's ok, even if you did, the kind of look you only got from an understanding mother. And then, as if reading my mind, she mentioned the hat. Your mother, she said fondly, knew exactly what I needed. She called me just a few days after Yun left us, not saying too many comforting words, just told me she had the perfect item I could wear to the funeral. The hat in fact. She told me about a small village in Valencia, not far from where they are staying, and the legends in those beautiful hats they made. Years ago, there were only mothers living there and no sons, as all the young men had left to fight a war they never returned from. Each time a mother received news of a son's death, she would shave off all her dark hair and weave it into a beautiful hat. These hats are legendary because the mothers would labour for years, weaving in fabrics passed down through the generations or treasured family heirlooms. And the deeper they loved, the longer their hearts bled, the more glorious their work would be. And then the village simply became famous for them. She sighed.

Holding my breath, I waited for the pieces to fall into place, but I was missing something, something crucial. I was missing the ending to their story.

"Aunt Ung, where are you and Uncle Ung going?" I asked quietly. Aunt Ung turned to me and for the first time in a long time, she smiled gently.

"We are going to find Ang. Yun found him." Here she paused and looked down into her lap, and I think she knew Ang and Yun's little secret. "He gave us his number and address not long ago. We thought maybe he would come back for the funeral but perhaps that was too much to ask of him. We have many fences to mend. But Uncle Ung is...willing." We all had fences to mend. Aunt Ung reached out, put her hand on my cheek and looked at me with such tenderness. In her face, I saw a thousand memories, my childhood, my best friend. Impulsively, I told her I was sure Ang would have wanted to be at the funeral, although I was sure of no such thing. It had been many years since I'd last seen him. He could have become anyone. There had to be, though, the hope that he had wanted to be present. Around us, suddenly, there was a change in the air. The rain stopped as abruptly as it had started and the air was heavy with its absence. We sat there together in silence for a while, until Aunt Ung let out another little sigh. She reached into her coat pocket and removed a small package, turning it over and over in her hands.

"Yun did not mention you in his will. But, he had this for you, to give to you, when we were alone." She passed me something rectangular in a paper wrapping. I looked at the package, uncertain, then looked back at Aunt Ung perplexed.

"I do not know what is inside", Aunt Ung said. "It was the only thing he told me to give you. He said nothing more, perhaps inside is the answer."

It suddenly struck me how flat and how long the package was, how small; and how Yun must have held it days, maybe weeks before he died. I wished I could smell his scent if I put the brown paper to my nose, or feel his fingers if I ran mine along the slightly bumpy surface. For a moment I thought I couldn't open it, couldn't possibly, but then I knew that I had to. So with hands stone-cold, I unwrapped the package and looked inside. And looked. And looked. His voice was in my head. He was here. And then for the first time since Yun had left me, I let the great wail always threatening, always present, just inside my chest burst out in relief. I put down my head, let Aunt Ung hold me, let her tell me it would all be fine and cried for the friend who had thought of me, always and only me, first and foremost, right till the end.

***

There once was a little girl named Lan, who lived with her parents up in the mountains, where winter comes early and spring comes late. They were poor and Lan was lonely because there was no one to play with. On a particularly bitter night, Lan and her mother waited long before the hearth because Lan's father was very late. Suddenly, the door to their small cottage blew open with the force of a thousand gales of wind. Standing framed in the doorway was her father and a stranger wrapped in a dark cloak. The stranger had collapsed and Lan's father had decided to take him home. Together, they carried the stranger over by the fire, laid him down and covered him with a blanket. At first he dozed fitfully but then he fell into a deep sleep, tended by Lan's mother. In the morning, when Lan woke, she heard noises coming from outside her room. Rushing out, she saw that the stranger was up and well again, and in fact sitting at their dining-table eating breakfast with her parents. When the old man saw her, he smiled at her and beckoned for her to sit next to him. The two fell into conversation, while Lan's parents went about their daily tasks. She told him everything. When Lan had run out of things to say to him, he leaned forward till his nose was just inches from Lan's.

"I have a secret to share with you, Lan", he said softly, his eyes twinkling. "But you must promise not to tell anyone. What would you do, if you had a friend to play with all day long, who would take care of you, be loyal to you, love you for as long as you needed?"

Lan's face shone with excitement, and that was the only response the stranger needed.

So the stranger gave Lan a kiss on her forehead, patted her hand, creakily got up and left the cottage. Lan chased after him, watched him hobble off down the mountain, his beard fluttering in the wind. Where is the friend you promised me?! she wanted to cry. As she turned to go back into the house though, her shadow cast itself across the ground and then it waved at her. Surprised, Lan jumped back, but her shadow didn't move with her. Instead, her shadow kept waving and started to dance around like a monkey would. Now delighted, Lan stuck out her hand and her shadow reached out and held it; hand in hand, the two walked away. From that day onwards, Lan was no longer lonely, because she had her shadow to keep her company. Lan's parents were surprised at the sudden change in their daughter; when they returned at night from work, they would find Lan tucked into bed, content, and not starving for attention as was her wont. As wisdom taught them not to question welcome changes, they kept their own counsel. As time is accustomed to do, the years flew by and the day came when Lan's father decided that she was old enough to go to find work in the village at the foot of the mountain. So it came to pass that Lan found herself waving goodbye to her parents as they drove off in their cart, a cloth bag slung over her shoulder containing several changes of clothes and some food. She turned, as was her practice, to speak to her shadow, when she realized that her shadow was no longer beside her. It took a moment for the realization to sink in as she swung around slowly, doing a full turn around herself. Then she gave a sharp, small cry. She looked down at the floor, but it was getting dark and she could not discern if her shadow was there on the floor once more. For the first time in a long time, she felt lost, lonely and bewildered. What had she done? Why had her friend forsaken her? Her heavy legs carried her to the nearest bench and she dropped her head down and cried bitterly over her loss, not knowing who she would turn to now. Even though the sky darkened gradually above her head and she knew she should begin to look for her aunt's home where she would be staying, she could think of little else but her friend. A cool wind stole over her as she hugged her knees to her chest and her warm tears fell to the ground. Somewhere she thought she heard a tinkle and the ringing of chimes.

"Don't cry, dear little one, there's nothing to cry about", a soft voice said.

Slowly, Lan looked up and saw it was the old man from many moons ago, hobbling towards her on a knarled old stick that was almost as knarled as he was. Quickly, with the back of her hand, she wiped at the tears on her face and tried to brush her hair from her face so she could look more presentable.

"Why are you crying, dear little one?" he asked, as he came closer and settled creakily next to her on the bench.

Lan looked at him, unsure if he was making fun of her now, because surely he must know!

"My friend – my friend you gave me", Lan said, trying to sound more thankful than accusatory, "She's gone. As soon as I came to this town, I lost her!"

The old man's eyes twinkled at her fondly, "Lost her? Now what do you mean by that?"

Lan gestured around her. "She's not here!" Lan cried miserably, "She's not anywhere."

The old man peered intently at Lan, "Are you quite sure?"

Lan hesitated a moment in the face of his intent gaze, before nodding carefully.

The old man dutifully poked around with his stick.

"Perhaps", he said, almost jovial. "But come, it's getting dark and it's not a time for young girls like you and old men like me to be catching our colds in this weather. Let me take you to your aunt's place." With the hand that wasn't clutched around his walking stick, he ushered Lan off the bench and towards her aunt's house. Lan was too surprised to protest – how did he know where she was headed? But the old man hurried her along, muttering happily to himself until they reached her aunt's small house. The old man rapped sharply on the door with his stick, stepped back and then turned to Lan.

"Dear little one, your friend may not be as far from you as you think", he said.

Before Lan could answer, the door swung open and her aunt stood framed in the warm light coming from the hearth inside.

"Lan! We were expecting you before night-fall!" her aunt exclaimed, sweeping her into a hug. After she had extricated herself from the hug, Lan turned to introduce the old man, but he had vanished. Lan glanced quickly up and down the street, but there was no trace of him, his beard or his walking stick.

"Where did he go?!"

"Where did who go, dear?" Her aunt said curiously as she led her niece into the warm house. Lan held her tongue as her aunt fussed over her, bundling her upstairs into one of the rooms, where the bed was newly made with old but clean sheets and soft nightclothes lay neatly folded by the pillow. While she changed, her aunt returned with a warm drink of mixed fruit and spices to help Lan sleep. In no time, Lan was tucked into bed, the moon-light falling across her face and the warm drink easing her into a

contented slumber, the old man and her friend hazy thoughts behind her eyelids.

The next morning, Lan awoke not a little confused. She blinked at the new slanted ceiling above her head and the noise of people just outside her window. The fresh smell of the sheets was different to the ones from home and the collar of the nightdress she was wearing tickled her neck. Most importantly though, she remembered and she sat up and glanced at the floor. In the daylight streaming in through the window, she saw her shadow there, and for a moment her heart leapt. But was this her shadow friend or just the silhouette of her lonely self? Was there any part of her friend in her own shadow? – She couldn't be absolutely certain. Disheartened, she climbed out of bed and went searching for her aunt. Downstairs, her aunt was busy cleaning up after breakfast, and Lan saw that her cousins and uncle had all left for work and school already. Lan's aunt herself left for work after a short while, telling Lan where she might try and find work and how to get there. After a brief bite to eat and then doing the washing-up after herself, Lan was setting out, determined to find a job, when on the door step she found quite different from anyone she'd ever met before.

"Hello!" the boy said and he seemed rather shy, with his cap in his hands. "Good morning!"

"Good morning," Lan answered haltingly, "Can I help you?"

"My name is Hua," the boy introduced himself. "And I live next door. I saw you come in last night and I know from my mother that your aunt has been expecting you."

"Oh!" Lan was mildly surprised. "Oh, well! I'm Lan!"

The boy smiled and immediately, Lan saw what an open, honest smile he had, how his lips curved up slightly more on the left side. "I just wanted to say hello", Hua said, still shy. "I thought I might walk you to wherever you might be headed this morning." He quickly took a step back, as if he might seem too forward with his words.

Lan's heart jumped as she closed the door behind her, testing it to make sure it was locked.

"I'm going to the town-hall. My parents sent me here to look for a job", Lan explained, her hand on her bag.
Hua nodded gravely as he put his cap back on his head.
"Lots of job opportunities here in town", he said proudly. "There certainly are." After a moment though, he added, "It won't be as nice living here as it would be living on the mountain."
Lan realized that the boy might have tried to find out something about her before her arrival.
"Have I seen you before?" Lan asked boldly.
Hua shook his head.
"I don't think you've ever noticed me; but I've seen you visiting your aunt in the past", Hua confessed. "I was so happy to hear you were moving to town."
Lan blinked at Hua uncertainly. His smile seemed to waver in her silence.
"Perhaps I could accompany you on your first outing?" he offered again.
Quickly, Lan looked searchingly at the ground – again, was that – or was it not – her shadow friend? – trying to understand what she felt; realizing suddenly, that she felt uncertain at this offer.
Finally, Lan nodded and together they set off. Hua found his new friend very quiet though, as she kept her eyes trained on the ground beneath them and did not volunteer any information, her responses were soft. He wondered if she was afraid of him.
And Lan thought, Can I trust him?
The sun rose overhead and crossed the sky, dipping again on the other side before Lan and Hua returned the way they had set out. Together they picked their way over cobblestones in the gradual dimming. Lan had yet to find work but Hua reassured her that it would not be long.
Hua left Lan at her doorstep with a friendly wave and a promise to return the following morning. She watched him walk away and wondered briefly at the slight lift in her heart. What was this feeling? she thought as she pushed through her Aunt's front door.

A Painted Moment

"Lan! Back so late! We couldn't wait for you but I saved you some food, just let me...." Her Aunt's voice floated out to meet her from the hearth.

Her eyes adjusting to the light of the room, Lan froze to see the old man sitting at the dining-table, entirely at ease, his pipe clamped between his grinning teeth.

"Hello, little one", he winked.

"Hello", Lan whispered, as her Aunt busied herself with bowls of hot broth. Lan settled herself in a seat across the table from him, and though she knew she should be bewildered, she could not seem to find it within her. Instead, she found herself smiling again, her shoulders relaxing as she looked past the weathered folds of his forehead and into his twinkling eyes.

"How was your day?" he asked, simply.

Lan's Aunt placed a bowl in front of her, and moved away, dusting her hands on her apron, moving into one of the other rooms of the small house, a trail of murmurings following her around. Lan noticed that her Aunt did not seem to acknowledge the old man, nor did the old man seem at all perturbed by this.

So Lan told him. She told him about wandering around town, paying visits to the grocer's and the weaver's, enquiring at the tailor's and the bookbinder's. No one said yes but all had invited her to come back, so they could get to know her before making any decisions, which was something she thought fair, and did not discourage her as much as she thought it would. She told him about the warmth of the cobble-stones, and the smell of the baked buns as she walked past, the light bouncing off the ripples of the river that ran under the bridge that divided the town. Then, finally, she mentioned Hua and here she paused, as she was unclear what she felt here.

"I..."

"Yes?"

"I think he wants to be my friend", she faltered.

"That is a good thing, yes?" The old man puffed on his pipe and a cloud, smelling faintly of chocolate, wafted up around his bushy eyebrows.

She nodded.

He waited.
"Can I trust him?" she burst out. "Will he leave me? Like my shadow friend?"
The old man gazed at her kindly.
Lan stared at the old man, hoping for wisdom. But what washed over her instead was another overwhelming feeling.
"Am I being a coward?" she whispered.
He shook his head and chuckled softly.
"No, I do not think you are", the old man said. "But, perhaps..."
Here, he spread his hands.
"Perhaps you could be more generous with yourself", the old man suggested sagely. "... Generous with yourself and then, perhaps you will no longer fear."
Lan continued to stare.
The old man smiled and gave his pipe another puff, waiting again until she blinked.
Perhaps.
"And, little one..."
"Yes?"
"...Whoever said your shadow friend abandoned you?" His shoulders shook with silent mirth.
Lan held his gaze for a moment and then took a deep breath before she looked down to the floor.
And then she smiled.

***

"Keep the stringy bits."
I looked at Olivia, almost amused.
"The stringy bits are good for you. Don't pick them off", Olivia explained patiently.
So uncharacteristic was it of Olivia to say something like that, that I had to look around to make sure it wasn't someone else's voice I was hearing. I put down the orange I was peeling for her and pushed the plate towards her. She picked up a bit of orange and put it in her mouth.
"Sour?" I asked her.

Olivia shook her head.

"Not too bad", she said, swallowing.

"What time is the doctor coming around today? Do you know?" I settled myself in a chair by her bed.

"Pretty soon, I think. What time is it?"

"Almost three."

"Yes, he mostly shows up around four." Olivia shifted, trying to plump out the pillows she was lying against. I reached out to help her and she leaned back with a sigh.

"That's better." A flicker of a smile, like a cat licking a bowl of cream.

"How are you feeling?" I couldn't help the anxious note that crept into my voice. This was only the second day the doctors were allowing patients in to visit.

"I'm better", Olivia said, in a measured tone.

"You look tired."

There were four beds to the room but hers was the only one occupied. It was right by the window and the afternoon light lit her face weakly. Her normally oval-shaped face was leaner and more drawn than I could ever remember and there were suggestions of dark circles under her eyes.

"You mean I look terrible", Olivia answered. "And I feel terrible, but better at the same time." Her arms came down to rest on either side of her, demure.

"How was Will yesterday?" I leant forward in my chair, my elbows resting on the side of the bed. The flowers Will brought stood in shallow water in a vase by her head. Olivia traced a pattern on the starched white bedspread.

"Bewildered", she finally said.

I didn't say anything for a moment, wondering if she was going to continue. I pictured William, all six foot four of him, always slightly dishevelled with a proclivity to absent-mindedness, and a sharp intellect. He would have been cramped in the chair where I was sitting. Uncomfortable in the starkness of a hospital. Bewildered. Darling, he would have said, my darling, your hands are cold.

"I told him to go home", Olivia said. "I told him you would take care of me for a few days…a week or two."

I nodded, because it was the only thing for me to do.

"And I told him I felt at peace", she said almost wistfully. "And although he probably has no idea at all what I was talking about, he was extremely understanding and said he would be waiting for me at home." And then she closed her eyes and I fancy I saw the glimmer of tears beneath her eye-lids. I thought of the day she called to tell me about her engagement. I thought of the hundreds of flowers, the smell of frangipani, floating dresses, laughter, the sharpest images I had from her wedding. I thought of her heartrending smile, the way the gold of her eyes would light up; and imagined a man losing himself in them and then maybe losing her.

I got up to refill the vase with water.

"Rachel."

I turned to look at Olivia. She slowly opened her eyes and her body was still, as if she were holding her breath.

"Yes, Oli."

"I didn't tell him."

I bit my lip.

"He didn't know anyway", she said.

"Quite right."

"Yes."

I left the room quietly, vase in hand, searching for the bathroom where I could fill it up. I wondered if William was really better off not knowing? On the contrary, might news of the accident put more stress on their marriage? I marveled, not for the first time, at William's trust in Olivia, his willingness to lay his faith at her feet. Part of me hoped his faith would pay off. I found the bathroom, replenished the water, briefly admired the hydrangeas in full bloom and headed back towards Olivia's room. From down the hall, I saw someone linger at her doorway. The familiar silhouette turned out to be Chloe. Chloe had been almost silent the last few days. She had not come to the hospital that evening with the others as she and Sylvain had been talking elsewhere. But she had been waiting for me on the porch when I returned home that first morning. I was sure she knew what happened but she probably wanted to know how, more than anything, or even why. But there was no way I could begin to phrase what I suspected might have happened. But Chloe in her wisdom must have guessed. She retreated to her room and stayed there for the next two days, only emerging yesterday when I called through the door to tell her Olivia was taking visitors. I had not expected her to come. I slowed my pace and stepped into the shadows, unsure if Chloe wanted me to see her. I saw she had come bearing more flowers, holding them pointing downwards as she hesitated for a long while at the door, an invisible line drawn on the floor, through the years, more tangible with every hurtful word uttered, more divisive with every tear drawn. Then I heard Olivia's distinct voice, stronger now and pleased. Very, very pleased.

"Chubs!"

Chloe put the back of her hand to her mouth as she stifled a short sob. Then she walked in, flowers in front of her, that invisible threshold finally crossed. I sat down on one of the chairs in the hall-way, smiling to myself.

***

The boat was sailing away.

The boat was sailing down the little path away from the Ungs' house. I watched two work men stagger slightly under its weight as they tried to negotiate the curved path. Behind them, Uncle Ung bellowed out directions, arms flailing, distrustful of their handling. He spotted me standing at the window and regarded me gravely, then waved before turning back towards the house. I waved too, but I might have reacted too slowly for him to catch it.

"The door's gone", I said, over my shoulder.

I waited a while longer, fingering Yun's parting gift in my pocket, until Uncle Ung walked through the doorway and disappeared in the darkness of the house, the empty doorway now like a large, open mouth. I could see lights on in some of the rooms and it was not hard to imagine another evening in no way out of the ordinary. I turned from the window, crossed the room and sat down at the kitchen table next to Olivia.

"Would you like some tea?" she asked me.

I nodded and she got up to fill me a mug from the kettle of water she had just boiled. I will always remember that door, always that door. The removal of it made my insides churn again. How do you pick up the pieces of your life and go on living as you used to, when your life is no longer what it used to be?

"What are you thinking?" Olivia asked quietly, passing me a mug

"I don't know", I confessed ruefully. "I liked that door."

"When are they leaving?"

"Tonight, after our dinner. They should be getting on the ferry..." – I looked at my watch – "...in precisely three and a half hours. Dinner's in half an hour. I hope Chubs gets back in time so we can walk over together."

Olivia reached out to squeeze my arm.

"It'll be different, but ok", she reassured me firmly.

The thought settled around me like a blanket being shaken, the air beneath it billowing it out until it finally settles smooth and straight against the bed.

"I can't imagine this place without them", I said unnecessarily.

"There are many things that at first appear unimaginable, later become tolerable and then just normal", she answered. "You don't have to like it, now. Time changes so much, you will have accepted it before you realize you have."

And there are some things that time can never change.

"Chubs and I don't think you should be here alone after Uncle and Aunt Ung leave", Olivia said abruptly. It was obvious that the two, friendship regained, had been talking about this over the last few days. That day, I had given the two almost an hour as I remained out in the hospital hall-way, deeply absorbed in the unfolding pattern of the hydrangeas. Occasionally, I heard small sobs or exclamations, but most of the talking was done too quietly for me to hear. I stayed in the hall till Josh, Glory and Sylvain had turned up, demanding loudly why I was sitting there by myself; so I could no longer feign discretion. We found the two in the room laughing, with swollen eyes and clutching sodden tissues. I wondered if we would be like that when we were fifty, laughing and crying over something that happened years ago. At the sight of them, Glory started to choke up as well and Josh had quickly produced a box of tissues, explaining she had been crying all over the place for days now.

"Why?" I asked, taking a sip of the scalding tea.

"Because you need company."

"Who's going to keep me company?" I asked, skeptical.

"Well, if you don't mind, I think I may stay for a few weeks," Olivia said casually as she played with her rings.

"Stay here for a few weeks?"

"If you don't mind."

"Mind? Of course I don't mind, Oli. But what about Will?"

"I told Will he should do some touring. And that I would join him once I was ready." She regarded me calmly. She was increasingly calm these days; her eyes almost wistful.

"Did you tell him why you weren't ready?"

Olivia smiled faintly.

"Not exactly. I just know I need some time and he respects that. and for that – well, there is no one like Will for understanding; there is no question about that."

"I think that's the right thing to do", I told her.

She nodded.

We sat there, drinking tea until Olivia got up to go out on the porch for a cigarette, until Chloe returned and complained about the smell. I opened the porch doors wide, so she could stand out there while I talked to her from just inside, leaning against the door-frame. The air was cold but refreshing and I could almost see the beauty in the small red glow of the tip of her cigarette. I wondered what was at the end of her thinking, where that course would take her. Somewhere, a cricket started to sing and I heard the front door slide open and then shut loudly. A few moments later, Chloe came into the kitchen, pink-cheeked and breathless as she unwound her scarf.

"How did it go?" I asked immediately, turning to her; and Olivia held the cigarette so the smoke wouldn't blow in.

Chloe smiled, shrugging out of her coat, taking her time as she folded it and the scarf over the back of a chair. She felt the kettle to see if there was hot water still and then took out a mug.

"We had a lot to talk about, there is still so much to be talked about, just so much catching up to do. All so long overdue." Her voice was thoughtful. "And I feel the better for it…quite. Easier."

I wanted to ask more but wasn't quite sure what the next question should be, but she saw the question in my eyes.

"I don't know", Chloe said. "But I think being here is better than being where we were before, and that in itself is something."

She popped a tea-bag into the mug and poured in the water, smiling to herself again, almost humming. Her cheeks were still very pink as she sat down at the table; looking very much like her old self. It struck me how long it had been since I had last seen that expression on her face.

"I said sorry. For how I treated him. That's good enough to start with, I think", she finally said.

Olivia laughed out loud. About time, she said.

Chloe tossed her a look and then got up to walk out to the porch. She took Olivia's cigarette from her and then dragged on it. We watched her suppress a cough and then let out a thin stream of smoke.

"And I've come to a decision", she announced; and then waited for us to prompt her.

We were too shocked from the smoking to articulate, so she impatiently went on. "I'm going to take a break."

I wasn't sure if I was more shocked by the smoking or by the news that she was going to take a break, Chloe, the workaholic, always moving, always thinking about the next story. But Olivia was nodding away, like she totally understood.

"A sabbatical," Chloe said dramatically. "And to start off on the right track, I'm going to stay here for a while."

Somewhere, someone trips and a knee is scraped and autumn leaves are kicked up in the scuffle to the ground. Arms sweep low to scoop her up.

A Painted Moment

I look at the two of them, and think how they must have planned this these last few days, to step for a short while into the large shoes Yun has left behind him. Fill a void that otherwise might not fill properly. And perhaps this will be good for them too, until later. Just a little later. So I don't say anything, as Olivia fishes out another cigarette for herself, offering the pack to Chloe, who takes it after a moment's consideration. She does not smoke any, merely turns the pack over and over in her hand, until I say it's time we head over to Aunt Ung's, otherwise we'll be late and the food will be cold. She always assumes we'll be on time and is continuously surprised when we're not. We bundle up for the brisk walk over and I slide the heavy front doors behind me before we set out together, initially in step as we come off the front porch. I love this feeling, of stepping off together and somewhere there's an echoing tread of the three of us walking in sync.

"I've been thinking", I begin, breathing out a cold cloud.

They look at me expectantly and I wonder if I have the courage to go through with it. How many things in my life have I not pursued, out of fear? How many times have I given up, stepped back from the edge, chosen a different course, out of fear. Yun took a needle for me when I was six, twenty years ahead of me in his bravado.

"I've been thinking of calling Nathan Brooks when I get back", I say, quietly, as we walk up a slight incline.

Chloe gasps even as Olivia asks, Who's Nathan Brooks?

"He offered to buy Wiseys", I explain, almost bashful, "only two days ago. I haven't talked it through with my parents yet. But I might call him."

"Wait!...When you get back from where?" Chloe's eyes narrow. Always count on Chloe!

I reach into my pocket and pull out Yun's gift, holding it in the air before Chloe takes it and opens it out. She stops in her tracks for a moment before passing it to Olivia, who also looks at it without comment. I realize from the crunch underfoot that frost has formed on the leaves overnight.

It's from Yun, I say simply. And they both nod, as if not daring to draw breath; walking without any pause until we join the road that will lead us to the Ungs'. I say it simply, I realize, because I do have the courage to go through with it. I realize this as soon as I have the courage to voice it.

That feeling in my chest, I know what it is now, it's identifiable finally. Weightlessness. Without a shore, without a shadow, there is only weightlessness. The sky darkens to a deep purple over Yun's house. Somewhere inside, Aunt Ung is stirring a chicken broth with a long wooden spoon.

In every life. There is always a moment when what once was, is no longer, and what will come is no longer clear. This is my moment.

A Painted Moment

Author's Acknowledgements

I would like to thank my editor and publisher Gillian Bickley of Proverse Hong Kong for providing me with an opportunity to share this story. Thanks also to the Hong Kong Arts Development Council for their support. Thanks to Kendra Wan for taking the time to read the book and then designing a beguiling cover! Thanks to my ever-patient friends who ploughed through all the permutations, drafts and re-writes. Lastly, thanks to my family, who haven't laughed at me, so far.

About the cover-designer

Kendra Wan was born and raised in Hong Kong. She studied and worked as an architect in the United States before she went to The Netherlands for a degree in conceptual design. Her favourite activities include organizing, reading, web-surfing and re-organizing. Kendra lives and works as a creative strategist in an advertising agency in London.

Translations / explanations of non-English words

"Ba" (*Mandarin*): shortened version of "father".
Cheongsam (*Cantonese*): Traditional Chinese form-fitting dress.
Die xian (*Mandarin*): Chinese ouiji board.
Fengshuibagua (*Mandarin*): Feng Shui Plate.
Hou tou gu (*Mandarin*): Large Chinese mushrooms.
"Lai" (*Mandarin*): "Come".
Li Bie (*Mandarin*): Depart.
Men lan (*Mandarin*): Bottom part of the door-frame.
Mien Tiao (*Mandarin*): Thin, long and white Chinese noodles.
Mochi (*Japanese*): Sticky rich cake.
Qian (*Mandarin*): Joss sticks.
Sakura (*Japanese*): Cherry blossom.
Shochu (*Korean*), Korean rice wine, stronger than sake.
Tang Wan (*Mandarin*): Glutinous rice balls, a Chinese dessert.
"Ting zhe" (*Mandarin*): "Listen".
Tofu (*Cantonese*): Soybean curd.
Wonton (*Cantonese*): Chinese dumplings.
Zhang Yi Mou (*Mandarin*): Director of *Hero,* Jet Li movie made in mainland China in 2002.

Glossary

Converse: Converse-brand running shoes.
Drunken Master: a.k.a. *Drunk Monkey in The Tiger's Eye*, is a 1978 Hong Kong martial arts action-comedy film directed by Yuen Woo-ping starring Jackie Chan.
Golfie: golf-cart.
Hoodie: hooded track-suit top.
The Hulk, Spiderman, X-Men, Transformer: characters in popular science fiction films and/or comic-strips, some or all with the same name.
Spaghetti-os: Pre-cooked spaghetti, shaped like an "O", sold in a tin with tomato sauce.

CHINA, HONG KONG & South-East ASIA FICTION
PUBLISHED BY PROVERSE

Andy Carter. Bright Lights and White Nights. 2015.

Peter Gregoire. Article 109. 2012.
(Winner of the Proverse Prize 2011.)

Peter Gregoire. The Devil You Know. 2014.

Lawrence Gray. Cop Show Heaven. 2015.

Dragoş Ilca. HK Hollow. 2017.

Caleb Kavon. The Monkey in Me. 2009.

Caleb Kavon. The Reluctant Terrorist.2011.

Caleb Kavon. Paranoia. 2012.

Ivy Ngeow. Cry of the Flying Rhino. 2017.
(Winner of the Proverse Prize 2016.)

Jan Pearson. Black Tortoise Winter. 2016.

Jan Pearson. Red Bird Summer. 2014.

Jan Pearson. Tiger Autumn. 2015.

Jason S Polley. Cemetery Miss You. 2011.

James Tam. Man's Last Song. 2013.

Paul Ting. Bao Bao's Odyssey: From Mao's Shanghai to
Capitalist Hong Kong.

A Painted Moment

CHINA, HONG KONG & MACAU NON-FICTION
PUBLISHED BY PROVERSE

Jean A. Berlie. The Chinese of Macau: A Decade after the Handover. 2012.

Gillian Bickley, Ed. The Complete Court Cases of Magistrate Frederick Stewart. 2008.

Gillian Bickley. Ed. The Development of Education in Hong Kong, 1841-1898 as Revealed by the Early Education Reports of the Hong Kong Government 1848-1896. 2002.

Gillian Bickley. The Golden Needle: The Biography of Frederick Stewart (1836-1889). 1997.

Gillian Bickley, Verner Bickley, Christopher Coghlan, Timothy Hamlett, Geoffrey Roper, Gary Tallentire. Ed Gillian Bickley. A Magistrate's Court in Nineteenth Century Hong Kong. 1st ed. 2005, 2nd ed. 2009.

Major (Ret'd) Brian Finch, MCIL. A Faithful Record of the *Lisbon Maru* Incident. 2017. Translation from Chinese with additional material. 2017.

George Washington (Farley) Heard. Through American Eyes: The Journals (18 May 1859 - 1 September 1860) Of George Washington (Farley) Heard (1837-1875). Edited by Gillian Bickley. 2017.

Sophronia Liu. A Shimmering Sea: Hong Kong Stories (Winner of the Proverse Prize 2012). 2013.

James McCarthy. The Diplomat of Kashgar: A Very Special Agent. The Life of Sir George Macartney, 18 January 1867 to 19 May 1945. (Winner of the Proverse Prize 2013). 2014.

Stuart McDouall. All Agog In China. 2014.

Lt. Cmdr. Henry C.S. Collingwood-Selby, R.N. (1898-1992). Richard Collingwood-Selby (Chile) and Gillian Bickley (Hong Kong), Eds. In Time of War. 2013.

FIND OUT MORE ABOUT PROVERSE AUTHORS,
TITLES, EVENTS AND LITERARY PRIZES

Visit our website: http://www.proversepublishing.com

Visit our distributor's website:
<www.chineseupress.com>

Follow us on Twitter
Follow news and conversation: twitter.com/Proversebooks>
OR
Copy and paste the following to your browser window and
follow the instructions:
https://twitter.com/#!/ProverseBooks

"Like" us on www.facebook.com/ProversePress

Request our free E-Newsletter
Send your request to info@proversepublishing.com.

Availability
Most titles are available in Hong Kong and world-wide
from our Hong Kong based Distributor,
The Chinese University of Hong Kong Press, The Chinese
University of Hong Kong,
Shatin, NT, Hong Kong SAR, China.
Email: cup-bus@cuhk.edu.hk
Website: <www.chineseupress.com>.

All titles are available from Proverse Hong Kong,
http://www.proversepublishing.com

Ebooks
Many of our titles are available also as Ebooks.